Lucid DREAMING

Where Thought,
Memory, and Meaning Intersect

Written by
SRISUDHA MODUGU

Translated by
ELANAAGA

AF518041

BlueRose ONE.com
Stories Matter
NewDelhi • London

BLUEROSE PUBLISHERS
India | U.K.

BlueRose ONE.com
Stories Matter
NewDelhi • London

For permissions requests or inquiries regarding this publication, please contact:

BLUEROSE PUBLISHERS
www.BlueRoseONE.com
info@bluerosepublishers.com
+91 8882 898 898
+4407342408967

ISBN: 978-93-7542-494-9

Cover design: Anuj
Typesetting: Tanya Raj Upadhyay

First Edition: April 2026

Some 'Dreamories'

I have been acquainted with Dr Modugu Srisudha's stories right from her first collection. I was astonished when I read her *Dystopia*. Writing stories well is not enough; they become literature only when there is creative expression in them, which is their core ingredient. Those stories are like long sighs, with a streak of melancholy in them. There are few Telugu writers who treat "experience" as a character in their stories. For many Telugu readers and writers, "experience" and "reality" are like desk drawers – always handy, ready to be opened at any time. But that is not true. For many, only the material world is an irrefutable reality. A prevailing opinion in the literary field suggests that discussing the reality of what we can't see or touch is futile. For over five decades, I have been reflecting on human memories and the inner world of people. I understood existentialism through the same lens. A discussion about it is not needed now. However, there is a strong connection between Srisudha's stories and what I am saying. This becomes evident upon reading her stories. In the preface to his short story collection more than three decades ago, Gabriel Garcia Marquez mentioned that he had dreamt of attending his own funeral along with his close friends. After the funeral was over, he realised that he could not go back home. This unusual dream, he said, helped him understand not only his own existence but also the mental torture the South American students had recently been undergoing. Dreams are incomprehensible truths unknown to us. They are not only relevant to our life, past and present, but they also erase the frontiers and dividing lines. A fluid, flowing life! This flow is evident in Srisudha's stories. Among them, I liked the story "Sea and Ross."

Three sentences from an article I read long ago remain deeply embedded in my mind. A Buddhist visionary said to his disciple,

"The world you are seeing is not real."

"Why?"

"Because it is you who is seeing it."

When I read Srisudha's collection of stories *Lucid Dreaming* (Jagrutha Swapnam), countless thoughts resonated in my mind like a wind chime. The term "Lucid Dreams" is the key to these stories. It is a beautiful term, one that encapsulates my foreword. Some years ago, I came across a line Picasso wrote beneath his own portrait: "Imagination is the only reality." It is an unforgettable sentence.

At first, I wanted to write about each story. However, after reading them twice, I decided against it. Interpreting them wouldn't do justice, I thought. Moreover, it would be of use only if we touched upon the contents of the stories. But these stories are different. We experience them in various ways. They emerge from within us – either as complete or fragmented scenes – scenes when we travel alone by a train at night or when we sit in solitude. Such literary experiences cleanse many incongruities and inequalities, transforming our perspective on the world. As a result, we move closer to society and its people.

I don't mean to say that Srisudha's stories are not comprehensible under all circumstances (like her prescriptions!). These stories are a melange of wonderment, surrealism, memories and creative imagination. In other words, they comprise 'dreamories' (dreams + memories). One or two stories seem to be linked to others. All of them are our experiences, though we rarely recognise them as such.

Among all these stories, I liked "The Golden Tusk" most. It deserves to be translated into English and other Indian languages. I first read it when it got published in a magazine. While foreign characters in Telugu stories often feel misplaced, in these stories both characters and settings feel organically rooted.

Another remarkable feature in Srisudha's writing is that her stories are recounted, not written. Perhaps this lends them an impression of subjectivity to most of them. She visualises the stories effortlessly. Handling stories in this way is not easy. While narrating them in an unembellished style, Srisudha has also achieved charming brevity. There is diversity in the subjects of her stories but not in the narration style.

"Pari Alias Parvathi" is a standout story. It is interesting, narrated in a simple style. In most of her stories, the setting plays a crucial role. In fact, presenting such stories to readers requires both courage and confidence. I believe many writers fail to maintain a necessary distance between themselves and their stories. However, I noticed that Srisudha is conscious of this. Her personal, stoic attitude could be the reason.

All her stories are small puzzles. The text and titles are succinct. Consider these lines from "Celestial" *(Aloukikam)*: Sifu stood beside me. Sadness had disappeared from his eyes. His small shadow of light was visible in my lap. In such a situation, it is a great experience to have a friend beside you, savouring the infinite darkness, cold and silence. "In the same story, the following lines stand out as original thoughts of the writer. "*Ammu,* there are no supernatural experiences as separate entities. Those we are meant to experience come to us; we must experience them."

"Three Cats" (*Moodu Pillulu*) is another good story. I believe it deals with possession. A kind-hearted, affluent woman befriends Leela (the story writer), and wills her house and land to her. However, she entrusts Leela with the moral obligation of passing the property to her grandson should he wish to live in it. The woman has two most beloved and treasured cats – one follows Leela closely, while the other keeps its distance. The grandson arrives, signs the ownership documents and leaves. Now affluent, Leela decides to sell the house and land. The grandson, learning of this, chooses to return and live in his grandmother's house. As in all the other stories, Nature plays an important role here as well. The cat that had left returns later. But then, who is the third cat?

When it comes to art, no limitations are admissible. All arts enrich life in diverse ways. Until we grasp this, we continue debating the utility of art. Writers like Srisudha create literature that fulfils this primary human need.

The stories that are in your hands are like bunches of *modugu* flowers (a Telugu term for flowers of a tree called Flame of the Forest).

Thallavajjhala Patanjalisastri
Rajahmundry
26 - 10 - 2024

***

Enchantment of Celestial Experiences

Srisudha's literary ingenuity is such that she cannot write poems or stories like others, even if she tries. . Be it stories or poetry, her way of writing is unique. We have seen her rare and extraordinary poetic diction in her book, *Amoham*. The genre she had couched in *Rekkala Pilla* is singular. While the stories in her *Dystopia* are of one type, those in this *Lucid Dreaming* (Jagrutha Swapnam) belong to another. Such versatility in writing is rare.

Grafting extrasensory experiences onto the fascination of alien lands, Srisudha has achieved a marvellous effect in these stories. A strong sense of universality runs through this book. Nearly ninety percent of the names of places and characters hail from beyond the frontiers of the Telugu States. Notice these names: Peiyar, Cheva, Gana, Sabu, Bidu, Sadhu, Muju, Sifu and so on. There is no irrationality in this. Perhaps the writer's main intent is to emphasise that man is basically the same anywhere in the world. The truth that intellectual experiences and the constitution of the heart are nearly the same all over the world validates this opinion.

The opening of "The Golden Tusk" and the ending of "Bluefin," etc., are quite fetching. In stories like "Kajika," one can notice the fulfilment of hidden desires in dreams. Psychology, too, testifies to the veracity of this. Therefore, they became incidents in these stories. There are few writers in Telugu land who deal with magical realism effectively. Srisudha carved a niche for her among them, which is pleasing.

Srisudha, who treads new and unconventional paths in writing, can be described as a litterateur with rare talent.

Elanaaga

***

The Stories Within

Some 'Dreamories' iii

Enchantment of Celestial Experiences ix

The Golden Tusk 1

Divider 9

Kajika 17

Three Cats 23

Excerpt 32

Bluefin 39

Images of Saboo 48

Illusion 55

Frank, the Painter 66

Phantasm 72

Rabeera 79

Bonjour 87

Pari, Alias Parvathi 95

Eureka 103

Sea and Ross 108

She - Dasu 114

Castle of Albuquerque 121

Celestial 128

Blue Comet 135

The Golden Tusk

If this conversation with Saravanan hadn't taken place, I wouldn't have known about Periyar or Cheva, or gone to them. Sarasu aunt used to say that if we are destined to meet someone, we would meet them somehow.

"Maybe, nobody has asked you what you wanted."

"It's not their fault, Saravanan. I don't know what I actually want. This day, I want to stay with some people; I like them a lot, and feel I can't live without them. However, after two days, I don't even like their presence. This happens to me not just with people.

My interests, the places where I live and the things I want – all keep changing. It has grown to such an extent that enormous disquiet is slowly accumulating in me. I am losing trust on myself. Despite appraising the problem, a lot, I am unable to understand why I can't stay stable anywhere."

"Perhaps you are a tripper!"

"No, I don't like going places. Journeying is not my favourite habit. Nor do I like to meet new people or having new experiences. In fact, tours annoy me. But something happens inside me and prevents me from staying in one place."

My cigarette was about to finish. Inhaling the last puff, I said, "I want to know why all this is happening and who is changing my mind."

Saravanan laughed. "It is natural for anybody to have such restiveness, at least a little. If it is inordinate like yours, we have to give some thought to the problem. You should meet Periyar and Cheva once. I feel they will help find a solution," he said.

My predicament is a feast of fun for some people. A few even gave me advice like well-wishers, while others ridiculed me, asking, "What happened this time?" But Saravanan never gives advice or pass any judgements. I noticed that he never probes anyone's matters – not just in my case, but in anybody else's, too. He never tries to help others, nor harms them. He appears to be a very selfish man. We worked in the department of Population Board Statistics, and our seats were side by side. That's how we know each other. I never considered him a good friend or a great person. People would become fed up and move away from me. Saravanan, however, stayed with me like a rock. Seeing him, I used to wonder how people can live without thinking or talking about others, even for a minute. Until my fiancée Neelima publicly spurned and deserted me, he never talked to me.

On the advice of Saravanan, I came here searching for Periyar.

I was eager to describe the difficulty I faced reaching here, but to my dismay, the old man didn't ask any such questions. I was disappointed.

"It's okay. You may assume I am an old person. I am ninety," said Periyar, looking at me placidly.

I was startled by his knowing of what I was thinking. His age also astonished me as his appearance belied his advanced age. He looked at least twenty years younger than he was. With a silver anklet on his leg, a loincloth and a dirty shirt, he sat on the ground with knees bent. I, too, had to squat on the ground facing him.

"Snakes move about freely here. Don't sit on the ground," he said.

Without saying a word, I sat on the fibrous cot lying beside me.

"Until recent past, many people used to visit this place. However, we are not allowing anybody to come here now. The mountain god does not permit us to bring humans here. Because you were sent by Saravanan, you could come here."

"How do you know Saravanan?"

"He is a tribal who belongs to this place. He was reared here."

He didn't talk about Saravanan anymore. He went in and brought hot porridge. "Drink this. We have to walk a long distance tonight, and you need energy for it," he said. It was a bit pungent, but as I continued to drink it, it tasted marvellous. I felt like drinking some more of it.

Periyar said, "You should not drink it to the full capacity of your stomach."

The ambience was new. It was neither hot nor cold. Cool wind was blowing intermittently. Gentle sounds were heard as if trees were conversing with the wind. I never heard such sounds before that.

I slipped into deep slumber without my knowledge. Periyar was waking me up. His language was rather crude. "We must start before dawn; else we cannot reach there on time. There is a valley at a distance of four miles. Cheva comes to the stream which flows in it," he said.

I wanted to ask about Cheva, but obviating such a need, he started talking about it while walking.

"Cheva came searching for Periyar when he was nearly two months old. One of its tusks was shining with golden lustre. The tribals assumed it was a baby bestowed by the mountain god and reared it," he said.

"Cheva used to starve itself for two days before the death of anybody in the tribe. Tears would flow from its eyes incessantly. After someone's death, it would go to the jungle and return after three days. It would stroke with its trump on anyone's head when the latter asked a question. People confessed that they got an answer to their question. As time passed, they started believing that Cheva had some supernatural power and could predict the future. Some had taken advantage of this and spread rumours to make money. Thanks to the hearsay, new people started visiting it. As Cheva did not like it, it went into the jungle. It shows up once in a while. People go to the stream in the valley and wait for seeing it. However, it doesn't come across everybody. Some people would wait for it for days and return with disappointment if they hadn't seen it. Some used to catch a glimpse of it, but Cheva would go without making any gesture. It used to communicate with very few people, but ...," he paused hesitantly.

"Somehow, it is strange that after Cheva gestures to the visitors, they abandon the idea of asking the question. They would not go back happily either; they would have a feeling of intense grief as if they had known some secret of life. Have you come prepared for any kind of result? What is your name?" he asked.

"Seshu," I replied. Periyar seemed to have trembled as he listened to my answer. "It is all right. How does it matter even if your name is Seshu?" he said, smiling.

I was two steps behind him. Thin twilight was pervading all over. Periyar was treading barefooted, yet he paced fast. I wore hiking shoes, but it was arduous for me to compete with him. I felt we had covered a long distance. Slowly, we started to enter the valley. The twilight has changed to thin darkness, and a cold breeze surrounded us. The path was so narrow that only one person could walk in it. Gradually, darkness was settling in the valley. Periyar advised me to descend slowly. He cantered without any difficulty; he was used to walking in that path. Pausing intermittently, he looked back at me. I started getting pain in my limbs.

"How much more do we have to walk?" I asked.

“We have almost reached the destination. Look up at the sky if you are fatigued; the stars would give you energy,” he said.

How do stars give energy? I suppressed my chuckle. Did I come here unnecessarily on the word of Saravanan, I reflected.

“Misgivings don’t let anyone believe anything,” said he. Periyar was reading my mind. Not Cheva but Periyar would clear my doubts, I guessed.

While I was immersed in such thoughts, we reached a broad river. But for a faint gurgle of water, no other sound was being heard there. On one side, huge boulders appeared as if they were stacked by someone at an inclined angle. Periyar climbed onto one of them and stretched out his hand to help me. Though I had visited many beautiful places before, I had never seen such a serene place. It gave an impression that no humans frequented there.

Soon, many birds flew around Periyar and perched on him as if habituated to such an act. They were bathing in the river and flying away. Their sounds resembled some kind of light music. All that appeared weird to me.

I asked him, “Have you brought anybody here before?”

“No, I haven’t. Their desires, missions were different from yours.”

“Why did you give it the name Cheva?”

"It is the name of my childhood friend. She was lost in the jungle and was never seen again. She came in the form of this elephant, I thought. That's why I gave that name."

A herd of deer came, drank water, and left. After some time, a herd of elephants arrived. Periyar said, "Cheva is not there in them." They bathed, swam in the water and left. Those scenes were magnificent.

"Cheva may not come!" I said.

Periyar kept silent. He looked at the sky and closed his eyes.

The sky was filled with stars and appeared to be looking at me. Their blue light was conveying something to me. All of a sudden, I felt that my entire life was spread out in that sky.

I hurled stones at honeycombs in my childhood and ran off to escape the bees. I also chased the running dogs and hit them. Amidst these memories, I saw the smiling face of my grandmother, and her eyes asking me not to chase everything. I couldn't get the hem of her sari to wipe my tears. I saw Ramulu, who, in my childhood, made me sit on his shoulders and roamed around. He was now singing with a voice filled with sadness. My father, who had left us midway and my mother, who felt very happy for that ... I ran wanting to get rid of agony. I didn't want sorrow but hankered for peace. Anguish was overflowing in me. Saravanan was not laughing. He was looking at me and walking into the sky. Periyar and Cheva were walking in front of him.

I didn't know when I had slipped into sleep.

I am hearing the sound of sprinkling water. In the river, there is a small elephant, Cheva, with a light golden tusk. A ten-year-old boy, looking like Periyar, is standing beside it. Both are dipping and floating playfully in water. The gleam in their eyes is showing a scene so beautiful that no artist could draw it. They are as natural as trees and leaves. Ninety-year-old Periyar has become a ten-year-old boy! Then, who is golden-tusked Cheva? Is it an elephant or God? Does it really have supernatural powers? But do they need such powers? They are not bothered about pleasures, comforts, misery, darkness or light. They don't need to go anywhere in search of anything. They have preserved themselves.

I looked at the sky for relief. Innumerable stars were seeing me, Cheva and Periyar.

I closed my eyes. I didn't want to talk to anyone. Didn't feel like calling Cheva either. I didn't want to listen to anybody or go anywhere. Nor did I want to search for the reasons for my stability or instability. Let death and life be secrets or no secrets.

I felt that someone was hugging me.

Is it a reality, a dream, or an illusion? I don't know.

***

Divider

Gana, I shouldn't have despised you. I want to tell you that there is some selfishness in my loathing. While playing with kids in the evenings, I see your heart in their tiny palms and kiss them to my fullest satisfaction. I don't know whether I can explain all this to you!

A crow came cawing and perched on the wall. Its beak was holding a piece of meat. I shooed it away. The meat piece slipped from its mouth and fell in the backyard. Suddenly, a rat came and took it away.

Who knows who lurks and grabs whom!?

It is okay if life passes ordinarily, is not cheerful but sorrowful. However, carrying it as if we have done an offence is unbearable. It took long time for me to understand that there is nothing like right or wrong, and some unknown injustice lies behind committing a wrong. I want to come once to see you from near, hug you tightly and get rid of the burden of my heart. But for this, I don't have any other personal reasons like discussing or settling something, Gana.

Does everything happen as per our wish?

I had two more hours to pass and realised that waiting is a difficult task. Unable to control myself, I came to the railway station.

9:32 am

I sat on a bench in front of the canteen and lit a cigarette. Every time I come here, I sit only on it.

"Gana, would you give up this habit at least?" This was Ramana's last sentence when she left me. Strange it is that Ramana, who cherishes freedom a lot, doesn't recognise my freedom to smoke.

Whenever I come and sit here, Kumar from the canteen sends tea for me even without me asking.

Sometimes, Kumar and Ramana look similar. They know the needs of others even without them telling it. Apparently, they look as if they are not noticing others, but they watch and attend them. They are vibrant as if very busy, even though they don't have any work to do.

9:45 am

The lean boy, whom I recognize, is moving here and there carrying *samosas*. Perhaps they were prepared last night. They have a special taste. He never appears to have eaten them.

Observing his gait is my habit. His condition can be known by seeing his legs. When moving briskly, they appeared to have hope in life and want to achieve something, longing for something. Sometimes they appear to be walking leisurely, loving all the humans. Other times, they walked sluggishly, listlessly and uninterested in the surroundings. However, while coming to me, he walks in a stable manner. Sometimes he says, "Don't smoke those cigarettes, Sir," making me reflect whether Ramana had asked him to say those words to me.

Ramana used to walk carelessly as if the entire world was hers. Occasionally, when she held my hand and moved, her manner of walking would be similar to that of the very lean boy. At times when she reeled a bit, her hand used to touch mine, and I would feel that fondness was encircling me lightly.

In future, perhaps this fellow, too, will hold someone's hand and walk in a similar fashion. It would be a great relief if he doesn't trip when the other person's hand leaves him suddenly. Ramana would mock me, saying I don't know how to walk properly. "Can't you walk vigorously? Why do you move so slowly?" she would say.

Might she have known the peace I had experienced while walking like that?

10:00 am

Ramana despised me umpteen times; she loved me the same number of times. And both the things she did equally profoundly. I like her feelings she experienced freely. Perhaps I cherished her loathing more than her loving! She thought she was special and was eager that I should recognise the same. I don't know whether she was special or not, but my heart had some blanks that could be filled only by her. Also, I think it would suit her most! I should not have resisted when Ramana wanted to leave me. Maybe it made her more resolute to implement her decision.

10:30 am

Buddi used to sell guavas in the station. When alone, she would put her two fingers in her mouth and immerse herself in deep thinking. Was she ten years old? What does she think in that tender age? Her habit is similar to my smoking. Probably she wants to forget something like me! She doesn't come near me but observes me from a corner. If I smile at her, she would reciprocate with a similar grin and turn her head to the other side. She would run behind the very lean boy whenever a train stopped in the station, show the fruits to passengers and sell them. Also, she used to sway her hands at the leaving train as a gesture of goodbye. When I saw her on those occasions, she would smile, shrugging her shoulders. The arrival of a train and its departure were equally pleasurable to her. Whenever I come to the station, it is difficult for me to escape Buddi's glances.

There has been no change in this station since Ramana left me. She used to like the trains that didn't stop. When passengers peep out from the inside of the slowing trains, they watch those on the platform piteously. "Their glances are funny," she would say.

Ramana, must have travelled in a train that had passed this station without stopping. Perhaps she turned her face to the other side, seeing this station. Maybe occasionally she saw my house beside the station. Which incident could she have recalled then? The one when I bit her cheek on the terrace, or my incompetence? Maybe my inability to reach her expectations is tantamount to ineptitude. To be naive is inferiority; not just in Ramana's view but in all. But what wrong did I do that prompted her to hate me? There is some kind of fear and pain behind her eyes. I couldn't grasp it until now. Did she abhor me to hide something? Why do people whom we love excessively suddenly turn strangers more than those who don't matter to us?

10:50 am

Rammurthy was the station master here in those days. I would say to him for fun: "Why don't you disallow a train once, so that the commuters will stay back?" Maybe because of my innocence, he would smile strangely. Glancing with flashing eyes at Ramana, he would nod his head funnily. He went to Gujarath on transfer. He must have come back. Did he get married? Had he come to Sangameswaram station on transfer, where Ramana is staying? He might have even met her. Who doesn't like his funny, flashing eyes?

11:15 am

Goods train was placed in loop line. They need to do it for trains that are to come. What value goods trains have? They lie waiting at any place for days. They move after all the trains leave, like how a stopped life moves again at the mercy of somebody.

I gestured to Kumar for another tea.

Dust was rising due to wind blowing strongly.

11:30 am

A train's arrival was announced. I became conscious of the fast pace of my heartbeats. Will Ramana come? What should I talk if she comes? How will she feel seeing me? Will she recognise me, in the first place? Will she come in the sari of mustard colour with maroon border, the one I like the most? Whenever I hugged her lovingly, that sari would touch my face softly.

But why is Ramana coming after so long time?

Fifteen years! It is too short a time to forget her, and too long for my contempt to vanish.

11:40 am

The train's arrival time is nearing.

I think it is coming silently. Shouting "samosas, samosas," the very lean boy scrambled to the train. Buddi, too, went along with him to the stopping train. Kumar got up and set his lungi straight. Crowds were moving, pushing one another. They have to get onto the train and leave for somewhere. Maybe, for their work or for someone else's!

The train halted. I felt some unknown agitation. It has nothing to do with how long ago Ramana had left. Ramana herself is the cause for it. I walked despite the denial of my legs. My steps slowed down. Am I not willing to face or greet Ramana? It would have been better if this train hadn't come. Perhaps I don't want Ramana to know that my futile life was good for me! I need to daringly tell her that I had forgotten her long ago and don't need to meet her now or say anything. Can I tell?

Am I indebted to Ramana in any way for having touched her lovingly? And getting love and contempt from her? But what debt do I owe to her? She gives love to anybody.

After waiting for so long a time, my heart is revolting against me now.

Ramana couldn't be spotted. People who got down from the train were leaving, and the train was waiting for a signal nonchalantly. Why didn't she come? Has anything happened to her? Perhaps she decided not to come. I stood there without moving anywhere. The bustle started dying down.

11:51 am

It seems the signal was given, for the train chugged. The driver signalled with the green flag. Suddenly, I felt someone pulling my shirt. It was Buddi. She was staring at me, with her two fingers in her mouth. I enquired her with my eyes. She pointed to the tea stall.

Ramana was standing there. I felt as though my heart had stopped. All the blood was rushing into my face. If I had asked the stiffened muscles of my jaw, probably they would have told me a long story! My hand went to my head inadvertently. As if trying to cover the newly appearing baldness, I pulled my hair to the front.

I felt as though Ramana was glancing at me. Is she the same Ramana of mine? Who is the other one looking like me? She was not the Ramana whom I kissed, loved, and despised.

Somebody was standing beside her. He was the one with funny, flashing eyes. I felt as if time had halted. All of a sudden, everybody's appearance became dim. I didn't know what was happening. I ran behind the train like a lunatic. The awaited life of the railway station was guffawing. The face with funny, flashing eyes was drowning me in its bizarre laughter. I was gasping as though all the cigarettes that I smoked were crying.

"Gana," Ramana's scream was reaching my ears through the wind.

Will I have another day for me?

Even in that severe panting, I was laughing gleefully.

Ramana won't have any need to hug anyone and breathe a sigh of relief, or get relived from the heart's burden.

I jumped into the train in a jiffy. Before I knew what was happening, the train's speed picked up. I didn't know where I was going, from whom I was fleeing, and how far I was going.

Now, there was no need of meeting her, touching her or undergoing the torment of seeing her smile. Nothing!

My heart that was wriggling in pain, was getting lighter slowly.

Buddi must be moving her hands, looking at the leaving train.

12:00 pm

The two hands of watch met with each other.

Time stopped and resumed moving.

***

Notes:

Samosa: A fried South Asian and West Asian snack with a filling of spiced potatoes, peas etc.

Kajika

I tried to recollect since when my watch had been showing wrong time.

I assumed that my smart watch was out of order, and replaced it with an ordinary wristwatch. But that, too, stopped working. It looked weird to me.

I took out the smart watch and checked. It was showing 2 December 12:20 am. I tried to correct the time. It changed, but soon showed the same old time.

I wanted to tell somebody about this. But, they might think I was mad if they see correct time.

How many times had I kept quiet or closed my eyes, fearing they would think that way? I counted it innumerable times.

But where is the need to ask anyone? December elapsed eight months ago. Why is this watch behaving strangely now? I checked my mobile phone. It showed 2 December automatically.

Why, why is this happening?

*

I tried to recollect what had happened on 2 December. It was Shyama's birthday that day. He works in FM radio. I rang him up. Since I don't phone him except on his birthday or when there is some shocking news to tell, he asked anxiously, "What is the matter?"

"Did I wish you on your last birthday?"

"I waited for your call on that day. Since there was none from you, I rang you up at night. You said, 'I met a special friend, so I didn't feel like calling you. Birthdays come and go.' Your voice couldn't conceal its harshness. You talked sparingly and strangely. That day, I felt it was not your voice, because it contained inclemency. You disconnected the phone midway. There was no mention of it later when I met you. I, too, didn't broach the matter."

An ocean started roaring inside me. I felt as if a whirlwind had snatched me and made me vanish.

"Did I tell you who that friend was?"

"I didn't have the courage to ask. Your voice was so harsh."

There was no need to talk to him, I thought. I looked at my phone again. It was showing the same date as before. It was a Thursday. What had I done on that day? I reflected. I enquired in my office. They told me that I had taken sick leave on that day. I tried to recollect the task I had done the day before.

On December 1, SK, who came from India, invited me to a party with his family in a restaurant.

A server appeared very odd during dinner. He looked like a Mexican. There was a certain firmness in his eyes. His looks were unforgettable. Moreover, they were directed especially at me, though with a smile. I felt he was strongly shaking the burden inside me, so I became restless. He was exploring my interior. What arrogance, I thought. I entered into a dispute with him on the lame pretext that he had knocked off a spoon. I yelled at him, saying, "Hey, Mexican!" He stopped for two seconds without moving, looked into my face defencelessly in protest, and left.

It appeared an altercation to me; I felt agitated inside my heart. I think I lost my cool and talked a few superfluous sentences. There was a restlessness inside me.

I thought I had seen him somewhere earlier.

I recalled the grey wolf that was hit by my car a week ago. It got up after two minutes and, looking back, left with a limp into the snowy mountains. The Mexican's glance was similar to that of the grey wolf. How severely the wolf must have been wounded on that day!

*

It was 11 pm when the party ended. At that time, Montana looked like a frozen beauty. It is usual for grey wolves to frequent those mountains. Driving carefully on the bumpy road in the freezing cold, I came to the spot where I had hit the grey wolf and stopped the car.

I thought of getting down for two minutes. There was silvery white light on the trees. The moon was not visible in the sky; green light pervaded all over. I couldn't even lower my window glass because of a slight, natural fear.

Then, I saw that the Mexican server and the grey wolf were walking amid the trees in front of me.

Was it an illusion or reality? I thought. I don't know whether I moved the car or stayed back there!

*

It is true that I talked to Shyama on December 2. But what happened all day after I had seen the grey wolf and the Mexican amid the trees? I couldn't ascertain, however much I pondered. What is the significance of the forgotten day's reappearance after eight months?

Maybe I will know after I meet that Mexican.

What should I ask after meeting him? What should I talk about? I was uncertain.

I sent a message to my office asking for leave and headed towards the restaurant.

The people there told me decisively that no Mexicans were working there. A few people belonging to a Native American tribe used to work temporarily in winter, they said. I grasped that he was not a Mexican but a Native American. Most people there revere Native Americans. Some, however, look down upon them. I consider them special people; they don't like to habituate to civilisation. The restaurant displays photos of the best employees who have worked there on a board. They asked me to check it. I saw his photo on the board.

They said, "He is Kajika. He works for three months every winter. He belongs to the Cherokee tribe, hails from a small village in the mountains."

Was the incident that I witnessed on that day real?

Suddenly, I felt very feeble. I don't know how long I sat there.

*

I completed my work in my small, single-bed flat and sat in the balcony with a cup of black coffee in my hand. The moonlight was glowing. The wind of the Montana Mountains touched me gently. Below the balcony, kids were scampering.

This problem was not created by me; it arose by itself. Therefore, it will be resolved by itself, I thought. I felt some tranquillity in my heart.

I kept watching the full moon in the sky.

My phone rang and stopped. I didn't feel like getting up from there or responding to the phone call.

My eyelids started to droop.

*

Kajika, the grey wolf and I were walking into the mountains. That path looked as if it was touching the moon. Kajika took off his woollen coat and gave it to me. Three of us played in the Snow Mountains, and were tired. Kajika and the grey wolf dropped me at my home. After taking leave of me, they headed towards the moon. Moonlight was showing them the way. Pain and heaviness have intensified in me. All of a sudden, I slumped there and sobbed continuously. I don't know for how long I whimpered. Someone was singing a song. All the sounds were weird. It seemed as though some dampness of some notes was slashing inside, and the same song was making it light.

Cold wind surrounded me abruptly. The moon has escaped into the midst of the clouds. The sounds of darkness were clearly audible. A delicate voice was saying to me, "Nothing happened. Only your listening is remaining."

The night was passing. The moon came and disappeared intermittently in those mountains of thin, green light.

Three Cats

It rained heavily last night, accompanied by strong gales.

In the next morning, when I opened the back door and looked outside, the ground was strewn with broken branches from the pear tree. Fruits lay scattered all over the backyard.

Behind the yard, Sandra's house came into clear view. The first time I saw Sandra was when she came to me to ask for pear fruits. Some people are such that the moment we see them, their face appears replete with experiences. This impression is not merely due to their advanced age but because they had observed many lives closely.

"My name is Leelavathi," I said.

"I cannot utter those names correctly. I will call you Miss Lee. Can I take two pear fruits?" she asked, smiling as she stepped in.

"Why just two? Take more," I replied in a friendly tone.

There is a raised platform around that tree. She perched on it as if it were a spot familiar to her. Her face brightened a little after sitting there. I sat beside her.

She said, "I live in the house at the back. The owner of this house, Johnson, was my friend. Johnson and I planted this tree forty-seven years ago. We used to sit here, eat sweet pears looking at the distant sea, enjoying ourselves immensely." She appeared like an ebullient child as she spoke.

"Would you like some tea?" I asked.

She got up, plucked some lemongrass and asked me to make tea with it. Its sweet, citrusy orange fragrance filled the air.

That's how my friendship with her began.

Now and then, she used to come, sit there and chat with me over tea. She often spoke about the tasks she had done with Johnson, their friendship, squabbles, the house, the pear tree, the piano in her home, the songs they had sung together and the birds – birds that would return even after being set free. Johnson's name would almost always find a place in her conversation.

One day, she asked me, "Lee, do you know music?"

I replied, "No."

"I will teach you. Will you learn?"

There was no reason for me to decline. That is how music gave me an opportunity to enter her house for the first time.

In her yard, a tall mango tree stood beside the stump of another tree. As I walked ahead, two cats suddenly darted in front of me. Inside the hall, I saw four cane chairs and a small coffee table in the centre of the hall. A piano stood slightly elevated in one corner. Beside it, there was a window. Bookracks were seen on either side of it. Under the windowsill was a long, crescent-shaped sofa. Everything there seemed to have grown with her, carrying her experiences.

Even objects, perhaps, would turn artistic along with the people they live with!

She made me sit on the sofa, went inside and returned with a small teapot, two cups and biscuits on a tray. They reminded me of the tea party games of my childhood. I felt as though that play had become a reality. The biscuits were not very tasty, but they were okay because of the nice smell of the tea.

"Won't you stay here for some days?" she asked.

"My project extended more than two years, so, I won't be leaving anytime soon," I replied with a smile.

Unlike most others, she didn't ask if I was married or living alone.

After a brief conversation, she started teaching me how to play the piano. She demonstrated how to move my fingers on the keyboard, emphasising that all the fingers had to be used; she made me practise patiently, and I noticed some innovation in her method of teaching. Gradually, music became the chief factor between us.

The two cats started to come near me. One was black and the other dappled. They seemed to love me as much as Sandra did.

The black cat always moved around Sandra's feet, while the dappled one stayed in the hall, observing from there.

Their behaviour seemed peculiar. "If I weren't here, this black cat would find someone else's feet and live, but that dappled one cannot live without me," Sandra would say. I could not understand why she said this, but her special love for the spotted cat was evident.

I noticed that none of her neighbours interacted with Sandra. However, she was never bothered by this. There were no photos in her house. She would occasionally mention, in a vague manner, that she had a grandson named Miller who was a drunkard. "He doesn't know the value of life, never heeds fellow human beings, and wanders like a nomad," she told me. I could sense that, except for Miller, she had no one else whom she could claim as her own.

She allotted Sundays entirely to the church. On those days, she would be busy getting ready to go to the church. A beautiful hat, a matching coat and shoes, a bag with tiny multi-coloured beads glued to its outer surface, and a Bible that would perfectly fit into the bag. There was some elegance in those variegated things.

Sometimes, she would invite me to the church. She was conducting singing sessions for a chorus group there. Many people asked Sandra to teach them piano, but she would only smile softly and remain silent. I heard people say that she never taught piano to anyone. This made me feel that my friendship with her was exceptional. Now and then, she would bring me dishes she had cooked. Among them, the sweet potato pie was very delicious.

Gradually, I restored the path behind my house that led to hers. Sandra was delighted like a small child.

Occasionally, she would invite me to her house for wine at night. She mostly talked about music; her music was distinctive in those moments, as if slight dejection and a bit of solitude cruised together. I would often listen to three sentences from her in those times of our privacy: "Lee, I have got a desire. I will disclose it to you some day. You must fulfil it even if it is difficult for you."

I often wondered what her desire could be. 'Will I go away from here without accomplishing it?' I thought. "If it is within my reach, I will definitely fulfil it," I would reply.

But she never revealed her desire to me.

One day, Sandra slipped in her bathroom and fractured her thighbone. I got her admitted to a hospital. I visited her daily, and she would be gleeful like a small child. She talked about music and cats. I never noticed fear or grief in her. I often wondered why I always saw a childlike spirit in her.

I never inquired about her life or her family matters. That, perhaps, brought me close to her.

One day, her smile seemed feeble and weak. She asked me, "Lee, will you take me to the sea?"

I took her to the sea the same day. She remained quiet and serene for a long time. Her eyes gleamed, and a faint smile lingered on her lips. The sea seemed to rush towards Sandra and gently touched her feet. I felt as if the breeze was trying to tell me something, and I was overcome with sadness. I didn't dare to speak to her. I don't know for how long we sat there together.

Sandra passed away the next day. Her grandson, Miller, came for her funeral. How he came to know about her or who informed him, I didn't know. He had not visited Sandra even once during the two months she was in the hospital, and I didn't know why.

Two days later, a lawyer came with her will. In it, Sandra stated that Miller could stay in that house for as long as he wanted to. However, once he left it, the house would belong to me. I was astonished at this. Sandra had never discussed this matter with me. So, I was apprehensive of facing any problem with Miller in future. He, however, embraced me and thanked me for being his grandmother's friend all these days. He thought I was the main reason for her very peaceful time in the final days of her life. He wished me happiness, signed all the necessary documents and left. I noticed that he hadn't taken even a single item from the house.

His behaviour seemed strange to me. He was completely different from what Sandra had described him.

The black cat began moving around my feet, but the dappled one was nowhere to be seen.

My life, which had been normal until that time, took a new turn.

Gradually, my neighbours started calling on me one by one. Those who hadn't come to me when I was with Sandra were now giving me some baked food, and offered their condolences. They said they had remained aloof from me because of Sandra, and now I could ask anything from them.

I heard new things about Sandra: Sandra was not married, and she had loved Johnson. Johnson had joined the military, married some other woman, and returned. Sandra left her house, but returned upon learning that Johnson's wife had died. My neighbours called Sandra a foolish woman who didn't know how to live a proper life. Despite being wealthy, she clung to old possessions, they said. They also remarked that they hadn't seen such an arrogant woman.

In the past, these same neighbours dotingly praised me, calling me modern and wise. I had joined them for boating and shopping in a jovial mood. They told me who in the area was rich and how much fortune they owned. They behaved as if wearing expensive frocks and other branded costumes was a trivial matter for them. They invited me to morning jogs, informed me about property prices in that area and reminded me how affluent I was.

Just in two months, suddenly my importance grew, and I felt as if I was the most beautiful and intelligent woman among them. Time flew by, but now and then, I would recall Sandra's last day of life when she and I sat together in front of the sea. I stayed in Johnson's house until the court papers were procured and the dwelling became mine totally.

One day, I went to Sandra's house. It was replete with dust. The piano was covered with fine powder, and the entire place emitted a musty smell. An iota of thought stirred in my mind. That house was on West Palm, Florida, facing the beach. Its area was roughly half an acre. A small hope sprouted in me, and I was unable to stay calm. The desire grew, and I started to have dreams.

I called a surveyor and had the house's value estimated. I summoned a realtor. When he saw the house, he was happy. The old piano attracted him a lot. He asked me whether I will sell it too. I pondered a little. Meanwhile, the realtor estimated the value, including that of the old wooden articles. As the final amount was substantial, I thought there was not much to think about it. When the inhabitants are not there, what value do the articles have? He looked at me approvingly. I put the house for sale.

Within a week, Miller came. He was furious. He accused me that I committed treachery by sabotaging his grandmother's trust. He told me he will come and stay in that house and left again.

That night, Johnson's house was battered by thunder, lightning, and gales. By midnight, the storm subsided. I had a brief spell of disturbed sleep. There were some dreams in it.

Sandra was sitting in front of me and laughing. She and I were on the beachfront. Sandra was smashing the piano with her hand stick and hurling its pieces one by one into the sea. They were flying in my direction due to the force of the waves and hitting my face. My face was full of creases, and slowly it was breaking. The dappled cat bounced on me, scratched my face with its paws, and vanished.

My project is now complete. I must leave tomorrow. I opened the back door and looked outside. The fallen pear tree was sprouting again. I saw Miller in front of Sandra's house, with two cats beside him. The dappled cat seemed to have returned.

The documents to Sandra's house are in my hands. They represent her unspoken desire.

***

Excerpt

Nobody imagined that a baby like Ami would be born in the family. In my grandmother's view, however, it was God's decision. She used to sit holding the Bible for hours, but I hadn't seen her reading it. My father abandoned us when Ami was in my mother's womb. Mother became very feeble after Ami was born. She used to beat her dried-up breasts and cry because she couldn't feed her baby. After a few days, my mother also left us. Since then, Ami had been a big burden, like a ghost, to us.

I think we started calling Amelia as Ami since the time she was born. I was about fifteen then, perhaps. With a big head, tiny, thin limbs, and bizarre, fierce eyeballs, Ami looked odd. Her eyes made one wonder whether they held the secrets of the universe. Nobody saw her blinking, let alone sleeping. Furthermore, her constant crying as if she was ravenous must be mentioned. Because of it, not just my grandmother and I, but even my neighbours couldn't sleep. Slowly, Ami's wailing became a problem for the entire village. Some villagers advised us, without our asking, to sedate Ami by giving her sleeping pills. Deciding that her incessant crying was due to chronic insomnia, they brought a sorcerer. His name was Danthu. In fact, he would simply utter some chants in front of a person bitten by a snake or scorpion and claim his incantations would nullify the venom's ill-effects. Yet the entire village believed he could even ward off devils.

Danthu said Ami was born with a curse, and whoever lives with her would inevitably be beleaguered by problems. He finally concluded that there are frozen tears behind her eyes, preventing her from sleeping. He further declared that the only solution to the problem was to instil shark's blood in her eyes. The villagers insisted that Ami should be treated according to Danthu's advice.

My grandmother never trusted Danthu. She would curse him, saying his heart was vile and he doesn't know how to treat ailments. She thought that, instead of seeking his treatment, it would be better to live in a house far from the village. As one of her friends agreed to let out his house at the far end of the village, we found a short-term solution to our problem. Sometimes, my grandmother would sit beside Ami with Bible in her hand and weep. When sad, she would lament, saying God had forgotten Ami. However, when she was happy, she would say God had no one dearer than Ami.

As time elapsed, one thing became evident: Ami doesn't like anyone coming near her. That was the main reason for her constant crying because she would calm down when left alone. In the beginning, it was grandmother's responsibility to look after Ami during the day, while mine was to take care of her at night. I learned watching Ami from a distance. Unless it was absolutely necessary, I would not go near her. I knew that if I approached or picked her up, she would immediately cry nonstop.

For livelihood, grandmother became a housemaid in a pastor's house in the neighbouring village. She used to say he was a very kind person. He would come now and then to our house and pray for Ami. Now, I had to attend to Ami in the daytime as well. Grandmother said her work at the pastor's house had increased, and prayers became frequent, so she started coming only once every two or three days. It was fine for her to escape from Ami!

There was a deep gorge near our house. People said a man called Gopanna had dug the earth for years to quench the thirst of sheep, and created a stream in that process. Shepherds believed their sheep were safe in that valley. Whenever summer came, they took their sheep into that valley in flocks. The songs they hummed at night would be heard from the gorge. During those times, it seemed that some fairies were singing. As long as those songs were heard, Ami remained calm. A blue light seemed to emanate from her eyes in the darkness, making them gleam.

I used to take Ami in my arms and descend into the valley slowly. It became a habit for me to go into that gorge, sit with the shepherds and return. But whenever Ami cried, the sheep would be frightened and run helter-skelter. The shepherds said Ami's cry resembled a tiger's roar, so they asked me not to bring her there.

Summer passed.

Ami's burden increased day by day. My anger, too, aggravated, perhaps because I couldn't carry her due to her weight. Danthu was right: our troubles began with Ami. I lost my parents. I had no friends now. People stopped visiting us.

Even grandmother came only once in a blue moon. I thought my life would be better without Ami. I pondered how to get rid of her.

I went into the valley with Amelia and reached Gopanna's stream. I had never seen it so closely before. Maybe due to the recent rains, it was full. There were verdant trees and many kinds of flowers around. Small birds were flying. The ambience was very serene. No sooner had I reached there than Ami started screaming. At once, all the birds flew away. Ami's cries reverberated through the valley. I placed Ami on a nearby flat rock and let her rest. After some time, Ami stopped crying and began observing her surroundings. I walked back without stopping.

By the time I reached home, it was evening. The whole house was calm and serene. After many days, I could sleep peacefully. I woke up at midnight. There was no crying from Ami. Deep silence prevailed.

All of a sudden, I started hiccupping. It persisted despite drinking water and trying other methods. The hiccups originated somewhere deep in my body, moved to my abdomen and from there to my throat. Their sound was awful in that silence. Unable to bear them, I shut my ears. Now, it sounded like a groan. My whole body was shaking due to the hiccups. I was profusely sweating; I felt heaviness in my chest. It was as though someone was screaming and beating me from within. I experienced fright, followed by agitation.

What might have happened to Ami? Extreme grief overwhelmed me. I got up and headed to the valley like a madman. My anxiety intensified. I could hear nothing but the sound of my hiccups. "Ami, Ami," I roamed, shrieking in the valley throughout the night. I couldn't find the stream. Exhausted, I slumped to the ground, crying loudly. I didn't know when the hiccups ceased or when I slipped into sleep.

I walked as if drifting in the wind. Gopanna's stream was visible from afar. I ran in that direction and reached it. It was completely calm there. My mother was sitting on the large, flat rock. I felt as if the sheep standing around the rock were looking at me intently. Ami was in my mother's lap. My mother was singing a song, looking at Ami's face:

O baby!

Have you descended from the sky for us?

Have you brought moonlight from the moon

And chill from the stars?

How have you glided into your mother's lap?

For whom did you arrive into this magic world?

O crafty cat, don't come here making noise.

Tender-cheeked baby Ami

Is dreaming fantasies with lustrous eyes ...

Ami was smiling in her sleep. Her smile was magnificent, never seen before. Her face was so bright as if it had swallowed the moon.

All of a sudden, there were howls. Alarmed, I woke up. Wolves had come and surrounded Ami. Neither mother nor the sheep were there. Ami was looking strangely at the wolves.

Ami's head grew larger. Her eyes glowed with blue light, and the laughter that emerged from her face made me shudder. It grew louder and louder until it didn't seem like laughter but a wolf's howl. The wolves howled along with Ami.

My hiccups resumed. The wolves turned towards me. A chill crept up my spine, and made me tremble. I turned back and fled. I didn't know how I was sprinting. My chest felt like it was about to burst. No path was visible. The valley looked dreadful, but I ran deeper into it. I hit a rock and fell on my back. Slowly, I stood up. Some monstrous creature was approaching me in that darkness. It appeared to carry the darkness on its arched back. It came near me. I felt as if I had seen it somewhere before. Its body was covered in dust, emitting a strange odour. It wore no clothes, and its hair was matted into hardened plaits. It raised its hands towards me and clutched my chest with its long, curved nails. My body shuddered. I thought the nails were penetrating my heart. I felt as though I had closed my eyes tightly. My mind was in enormous confusion.

Without any conscious effort, I said Ami was missing. It seemed like an explanation. I was aware that my throat was so choked that the words barely came out.

It opened its mouth, and a gurgling sound emerged. "Where are you searching for Amelia? Is she inside your heart, or outside? Will the Ami whom you stamped under your feet leave you? Will your hiccups that are similar cease?" it said in a harsh voice, pushed me and disappeared into the darkness. My body was turning into a lump of ice. A large void was forming. I felt as though I was losing myself.

*

Sunshine singed my hand. I opened my eyes and saw the roof. Ami was crying beside me. I heaved a sigh of relief. The sides of my chest ached as if they had shaken violently in the night. There were marks on my chest as though someone had pressed it hard.

***

Bluefin

Rock stays in Columbus. Though Albert Creek Lake is a bit far from his residence, he likes it immensely. He has been going there for the last two months with great enthusiasm. He is waiting for such a chance even more eagerly. Teju called and informed me that a girl would come there and asked me to meet her. She also said, "She is a bit freaky. So, be cautious." But she did not disclose the girl's name. As if giving a hint, she added: "If you succeed in making her reveal her name, think that she has accepted you as her friend." Teju is Rock's only Indian friend.

***

He saw her coming in his direction. She was wearing a hoodie, walking as though leaping a bit in the air. Her eyes were smiling peculiarly. There were two or three types of bracelets on her wrists. He wanted to go and greet her with a smile, but meanwhile, she came and sat opposite him.

He remained silent for some time, for he didn't know what to say. She started the conversation.

"Isn't it very pleasant here?"

"Seashores are always nice."

"Where is sea here?"

"Aren't you in front of me?"

Is he flirting? It appears so. Let him. This, too, is nice to some extent, she thought.

***

I didn't want to extend the conversation. Teju asked me two or three times to meet him. It was all set today.

He continued: "Do you come here frequently?"

"Not frequently, but I come whenever I get time."

"Alone?" I understood what he wanted to ask. I didn't feel like giving any reply.

"Isn't the sunset very gorgeous here?"

"Yes."

"Please don't consider me a stranger. I work for Bank of America downtown."

Would he stop being a stranger if he told where he was working? Maybe he wants to tell that he is the most trustworthy among strangers! What if he is trustworthy? Is it for continuing the dialogue, having coffee together, and camping, if possible? His colloquialisms indicated that he was a Mexican. Like Indians, they too come to this country and go through hardships. They don't have time to cheat others. But should a chance arise, they don't look for major reasons!

As I was immersed in my thoughts without talking, he asked what my name was.

I said, "Is name that important?" I smiled.

"But shouldn't we call people by some name?"

"Then, call me by some name. No problem for me."

"Can I call you Lucy? No special reason for it; it's the name of a girl who lives in my neighbouring house."

"Oh! I thought it is your puppy's name," I said, making it sound like a joke. He said, "No." It seems he hasn't taken it as a joke.

"You can call me Rock," he said again.

I thought of asking, 'What rock?' But I refrained from doing so because it looked unnecessary prolongation.

He said, "I come here along with my younger brother for fishing. Shall we walk?" He advanced ahead without looking at me.

I looked at him for a few moments in an examining manner. He had a rugged shirt, dishevelled hair and a small, smiling face. Lips appeared as though they were about to say something. I felt I had seen him somewhere earlier.

"Are you coming, Lucy?"

Rock was talking to me as if he had known me for aeons. Many kids, swimmers, anglers, and boatmen were there. They were playing, revelling and enjoying themselves there.

"I have been coming here every weekend for one thing," he said while walking. "About two months ago, once when it was six in the evening ..." He paused, looked at me, and resumed walking. He wanted to insinuate suspense in the middle of his talk.

He was leading me into the midst of big rocks, away from the crowd. 'Do I have any costly articles with me?' I reflected. My own thought made me chuckle.

"Are you often used to soliloquy!?"

"No, not at all. Why to go still farther?"

"It's all right, Lucy. Let us go a little farther. It will be nice there. This whole place is safe."

We climbed a big boulder and proceeded further. I knew that place would be nice. He was telling as if he had discovered it.

"Come, let us sit here," he called me onto a boulder that was a bit flat. If one sits on it, the rushing waves come, touch the feet and return.

"How nice is this place? The sunset looks beautiful from this point."

I reminded him that he was about to say something, but didn't say it.

"I will tell you about it after the sunset," he said, and suddenly glanced at me. "I feel you are known to me for a very long time," he added.

I kept quiet.

After a few moments, he started enumerating his hardships. First, he described his lover who had deserted him, and later recounted her worldly shrewdness. He abused her and grieved. He accused her of cheating on him.

"Why don't you talk, Lucy?" said he.

"Did you truly love your lover?"

"I thought my life would be delightful with her. Of course, I don't regret much for her leaving me. By deceiving and deserting me, she saved me from pain. She left a reason for me to show." he mumbled, pondering.

"Or were you afraid that your inability to love her would become evident?" I laughed loudly.

"Did you love anybody?" he asked me presumptuously.

"I did, many times," I replied. He was dismayed. I thought he would be distraught if I talked more. He recollected his mother for some time. He said she would wait for him even if it was late at night, always be anxious about him, and love him greatly. He wanted to emphasise that she was a very nice and unselfish person.

"So, you love your mother!"

"Who doesn't love his or her own mother?"

"I don't know," I said.

"Don't you love your mother?" his question was direct.

I thought he was ready to see a cruel woman in me if I didn't love my mother.

"I don't know," said I placidly.

"Why so?"

"I never pondered if I should love my mother or not."

Our conversation drifted to his lover and stopped at his mother.

"You haven't told anything about yourself."

"I don't stay anywhere stably. Currently, I am staying at my mother's friend's. I roam with a bike-riders group. I don't have any aims. All I want is that my life should move ahead without any tedium."

"Oh! Why so?"

"Staying in one place fixedly, loving own people and grieving for them ... I don't like all this. Sometimes I feel that, unable to bear or fill their emptiness, people load their lives with love and pain."

The glance that he flung towards me was quite amusing.

"What? Haven't you loved anyone?"

It was a relief for me that he hadn't asked me about my mother; he just wanted to know if I had any lover.

"I don't know if I had done so. There was one man called Martin in our bike-riders group. Once, we went on a trip to the Grand Canyon. During that time, he always used to be with me, even offer to help me with trivial things. He would ensure that I am always comfortable. Slowly, I started depending on him. He would listen to my words with great interest and attention. Rarely, he said that my smile was lovely, and that I could talk with my eyes. What he wanted has happened; I started liking him immensely. I could not bear it if he suffered the slightest injury. I would fight against anyone who tried to hurt him with words. The aplomb in me gradually started dwindling. Everyone in our group noticed the change in me, yet pretended as if they hadn't.

Unable to withstand even the slightest gap, he said, "What happened next?"

"Once, his leg was injured a little in a bike accident. Despite his request that I should proceed, I stopped and stayed with him. In that night ..." I paused.

Rock looked at me intently. His glances were saying, 'No problem, go on.'

"Saying that he was highly distraught, he asked me to lie beside him. I thought there was nothing objectionable in it. I slept by his side as if waiting for it. He suddenly snatched my hand so tightly that it pained. Then, he kissed me madly. It made me ecstatic. I knew that I liked it. But he held my hand so tightly that blood flow was impeded, and it turned blue. Mustering all my power, I pushed him aside and got up. I ran without looking back. After that, I never indulged in the thought of love."

"Didn't you think of meeting Martin again?"

"Don't you know that if blood flow stops, death could occur?"

Had the Bluefin not arrived, our conversation would have ended there.

Twilight spread around. There appeared a small quest in him.

"Why are you somewhat disturbed?" I asked.

"I used to hear various kinds of sounds here. At the beginning, I couldn't make out where they were coming from. At last, I realised that they were coming from the water. Then I saw the Bluefin fish. It was so magnificent that I couldn't divert my eyes from it. I could discern that it was making those sounds and trying to communicate with me."

I bent forward with inquisitiveness.

"The Bluefin arrived at the spot between the rocks, went back, and returned. It was stunningly awesome. Slowly, it familiarised itself with my presence and came near my feet. Seeing it, I was ecstatic. After staying near my feet for some time, it went back into the water."

After a short interval, he related the events again. "I saw it for the first time on the day my lover deserted me. Watching it, I forgot my torment. I have been spending my time here every day for a few hours."

"Do fishes listen to us?"

"I don't know, but gradually, I started comprehending its sounds. I realised that it was singing. Its song was so vehement that sometimes I would cry. At other times, exhilaration would surge from within me. On those occasions, it appeared as if it was chanting a peace mantra. I used to forget people and surroundings. I liked that Bluefin so inordinately that once I wanted to take it home. Strangely, the moment that thought came to my mind, it stopped its song at once, as if it had read my mind. The next day, I apologised to it in my mind and waited for it. Then, it appeared again. It was very queer to me. I felt it was telling me that we like and love anyone or anything only till we don't own it; there is a discomfort in the very thought that something is ours."

"Do you mean that no such discomfort would be present after owning something?"

"Yes. Except selfishness, nothing would be there." There was firmness in his voice.

Glancing at me, he said, "Lucy, what I am saying is true."

"I agree with you," I said, looking at the water.

After a brief silence, he asked me, "What is your name?"

I was amused. I looked into his eyes and smiled faintly.

I was aware of the Bluefin's movements around my feet.

***

Images of Saboo

Harry came to my mind immediately after I got out of my dream. I thought he would analyse my dream if I narrated it to him. However, he talked puzzlingly about himself and left. After that, however much I wanted to meet him, I never came across me.

I used to meet Harry in this park on and off when I came here for walk.

His introduction to me was strange.

Once, when he was walking here, I noticed that currency notes were falling down from his pocket. Going behind him, I picked up all the notes and placed them in his hand.

Looking sadly at me, he said, "Why are you giving them to me? They want to depart from me."

"They are not thinking of leaving you. It's only you desiring so. However, nothing would leave us just because we want it to! They leave us only when they want to do so. This is especially true in the case of money." Laughing, I put them in his hand.

That is how Harry and I got introduced to each other. Whenever I thought of Harry, he used to appear before me at once. It was very weird. If I asked how he can appear in front of me at once whenever I think of him, he would reply that it is because I wanted him to be with me. It looked as though he was saying it seriously. "Won't you come if I ask you not to?" I used to ask him derisively. Harry would smile and keep quiet. He would talk about many things. His words had no connection to human beings.

One day, I told Harry that I had a dream the previous night.

"You never talked about dreams. Do you believe in them?" he asked.

"Of course I don't. Some dreams dupe us, while others tell lies that all people are good. Sometimes, I dream of moving with someone, and that person taming me. I get scared. Most often, I don't remember the dreams I get. They come and go like magic. That is why I don't believe in them, and I don't care for them. But this one is not of that type. It is very bizarre."

Usually, Harry listens to me attentively whenever I tell him anything. After listening, he talks a little. Very rarely, he talks to me exhaustively without observing whether I was listening to him. This time, however, he kept quiet even though I talked in detail. He seemed to be totally immersed in some thoughts.

After some time, I started narrating the dream:

"I was wandering in trees like a green snake ... hopping from one tree to another. My body was soft and green. Also, it was light because it had no vertebrae. How nice it is if one doesn't have vertebrae!? We can coil around anything. I was entwining my body around the tree branches and meandering amid them. Occasionally, I was flying. I was happy that I was well-camouflaged in the trees; nobody was seeing me. I felt I need not be frightened, for I was not a human being. An eagle saw me from above and swooped down to catch me. Sensing that it was reaching me, I was terrified and fell down to the ground. I turned into a human being immediately and ran. The eagle that had been chasing me flew away. I felt dejected for becoming a human again. I wept bitterly in the dream. Then, I woke up."

Harry's face displayed agitated laughter. "What happened?" I asked.

After hesitating for some time, he said, "I need to tell you one thing." Then, he paused for a while.

I fathomed that he was about to say something impertinent without talking about my dream. I had never heard Harry telling about himself. Hiding my eagerness, I maintained a normal facial expression.

He glanced at me once. His eyes were similar to clouds before rain. I thought he was going through a conflict inside his heart.

He said, "Of late, I have been very thirsty. No amount of drinking would quench my thirst. As the water I had was insufficient, I asked in other houses for some more water and drank it."

"You should have consulted a doctor," I said, though my advice seemed odd and absurd to myself.

I think what I was listening to did not conform to what he was saying. He was recounting continuously without listening to what I said.

"My thirst was unquenchable. It was intensifying and burning me inside. After some days, I had insomnia. I consulted a psychiatrist. He said that the symptom is called polydipsia, and confirmed that I was suffering from a type of schizophrenia. I was scared. I tried to explain to him that I had no other problem except excessive thirst. But he refused to agree. He prescribed some sedative drugs for me. However, I didn't use them. I never consulted any doctor again. My thirst went on increasing. One night, unable to withstand the thirst, I wandered outside like a madman. After rambling for long, I was exhausted and sat under a tree. A few drops of water dropped from the leaves above, and they fell on my lips. I felt that the fire raging in my stomach was doused by the water drops. I went on drinking drop by drop. My thirst was quenched for that day. Maybe because my chronic thirst had vanished and my exhaustion ceased, I slept there like a log of wood."

I was listening, flabbergasted. His words frightened me.

"Do you still have that problem?" I asked anxiously and hesitantly.

“Yes. In the beginning, just two drops of water sufficed. However, now unless I drink one drop more than the previous day, my thirst is not quenched. That way, the number of water drops that I need to drink is increasing day by day. What is more peculiar is that after drinking water falling from one tree, that tree is drying up slowly.” His voice trembled a little.

“Is this a dream?” I asked with suspicion.

“Saboo, how can we say what is dream and what is reality? Tell me whether you are in a dream or in reality now,” he questioned me.

I felt a bit befuddled. I asked, “That means are you not a reality now?” Harry gave forth a faint, mysterious smile.

His recounting seemed odd to me. I wanted to describe my dream to him, but he was narrating one to me! Why? I pondered. I grew sceptical whether my dream is real and this Harry, who always looked real, is a dream.

Becoming a little stable, I asked, “How many drops do you need now?”

“I need half of the trees in my garden! When I enter my garden, all the trees are whispering to one another. They are getting terrified as if I am a sorcerer. I don’t know how to get rid of this problem of thirst, Saboo,” he said woefully.

His skin had thin creases, and it glowed with a light-yellow tint. Harry never tells lies. His torment was clearly visible in his eyes.

Wanting to divert his thoughts, I reminded him of my dream. I said, "Do you know that there is no venom in green snakes?"

Harry grew pensive and said, "My grandfather used to say that they bite in the eyes of human beings."

I felt as if his words boomeranged. "How can you live if there are no green trees?" I asked with exasperation.

Without giving any heed to my question, he said, "I don't think snakes are bad," and left.

I didn't expect that our conversation would end so absurdly and abruptly.

Of late, I am feeling that the trees in that garden are drying, and their bark is coming off in bits. I understood that what Harry had told me was true. I reflected on what should be done to diminish Harry's thirst. I didn't get any answer. I thought that because of Harry, the intensity of summer was increasing. I was terrified at the thought that the entire world might turn into a desert. Harry was drinking every drop of water from the air, I thought.

I cursed myself for having befriended him. I wished repeatedly that he should die. That night, my heart became despondent all of a sudden. Soon, I experienced maudlin joy too.

The next day, a terrible storm ensued. It rained cats and dogs for three days. The sun was not to be seen. Most of the trees fell as if the lower parts of their stems were hacked. The situation was a bit better after one month. Trees were sprouting, and there was lustre of life in them. They looked fresh, too.

Imagining that Harry had disappeared from the world, I felt immense joy. I consoled myself, saying that he didn't vanish because I wanted it, but he had done so because he didn't want to stay on the earth. I was happy because the world was saved, not because Harry ceased to exist.

After a few days, I noticed that the nail of my pinkie had started turning green!

***

Illusion

Since my grandmother disappeared from my life, I used to torment myself in the process of not allowing her to escape from me. Had Lacchimi not met me, perhaps I would have borne grandmother as a huge burden.

I know my grandmother liked the bank of the Krishna River. I don't know why she had come to this small village or what she got here. She left all her people, came here alone and started living in this house. She never allowed anybody to come ... not even me! She might not have imagined how much it pained me; later, it transformed into anger.

Maybe she wanted me to be informed of her demise. He apprised me of the news. I was reared at grandmother since my childhood. However, I did not weep when I learned that she had died. What must I have lost!? None of the few relatives she had come for her funeral. He oversaw all the rituals perfectly.

His name is Nandi. It sounded strange to me.

The tiled house comprised just two rooms with two pials in the veranda. A nylon-strapped chair and a wicker cot were there as well. Apart from her kitchen utensils and saris, the small, multi-coloured bamboo baskets and tiny variegated cowries in them were more attractive. A trunk box was lying beside dolls made with cowries. I didn't want to open it. They all suggested how much grandmother was fond of that house. Despite reflecting for long, I didn't understand why she had left everybody and how she stayed alone in this house for so long. I felt as if I was carrying someone's weight and that some secret was eluding me.

Can I stay here for eleven days?

But that night's dream and the ones that repeatedly pursued me changed everything.

The first dream was perplexing and vague:

There are many herds of goats in the green hills. Children are playing there. One of the kids is appearing exactly like me. With shining eyes, she is looking at me on and off and laughing intermittently. After playing for some time on the trees, they are opening their food containers. But that child was not seen anywhere. 'Lacchimee,' someone is calling her. Afar, a child is climbing a hill and looking back. I understood that she is Lacchimi. I also bellowed, 'Lacchimee!' She turned to me, smiled weirdly and vanished into the hills. I think I woke up screaming her name.

I hardly get dreams. Even if I do, I can't recollect them later. When grief, happiness or some unknown agitation stirs in me after I wake up in the mornings, I surmise that I might have dreamt in the night. This dream, however, was vivid though its beginning was vague. I felt unusual.

Nandi hardly talked except for, "Venamma, shall I bring anything for you?" and so on. He would be perhaps thirty or thirty-five years old. He is tall and thin, yet looks strong. His complexion is black. It is mixed with green tint, rendering it somewhat nondescript. His fingers and toes are long. He ties his long hair transforming it into a chignon. Whenever he walked, it appeared as though some thin layer of light was moving around his body.

He used to come from riverbank. He told me that he had a small raft and ferried people between the two banks of the river. He attended to everyone's needs. He brought everything I asked for.

Who is this man? Has he been helping my grandmother like this for the past ten years?

As I was tired on the second day, I slipped into sleep early. I don't know what time a dream started. Lacchimi appeared in it again. She was climbing trees, jumping down from them, going near a waterfall, getting wet there and laughing loudly. The bleats of goats were heard. She came walking through the water. Goading a herd of goats, she reached the children and mingled with them. All of them are descending the hill. There were homesteads at the bottom of the hill. Walking slowly behind the goats, Lacchimi was looking at me and inviting me to her house. After waking up, I realised that the previous night's dream had some connection to this one. My third night's dream validated this suspicion. Lacchimi's plays, kids, goats, forest, waterfall and flying birds ... all appeared again. In the fourth night's dream, Lacchimi took me with her wherever she went. I, too, climbed up trees along with her and jumped down. I liked our running to the waterfall, and playing under the water.

I used to feel that these dreams were carrying me with them, and I actually I lived those moments. They appeared to have been continuing for years.

Do dreams give so much delight?

I used to feel that I had seen Lacchimi before – silver rings on her ankles, a short hand stick with tiny bells at its upper end! With shining eyes, she would run without stopping. She used to occupy my thoughts even in the afternoons.

I like this tiled house now. Its surroundings and ambience are no more new to me. The whole place appeared eternally familiar.

Nandi is coming and going daily, attending to my needs with concern. He appeared to have noticed my joy. Now, I know that I am waiting for nightfall and a dream.

I tried to sleep but was unable to do so for a long time. I kept tossing to either side for quite some time. I got up and sat on the bed in that darkness. After some time, I opened the window and saw a white owl outside. It flew away as I opened the window. Frightened, I screamed.

Someone was knocking at the door. When I looked at the clock, it showed four in the early morning. Who could have come so early? I had no idea. I opened the door. It was Nandi. Suppressing my inner angst, I asked him, "Why have you come so early, Nandi?"

He said, "It is full moon day today. The riverbank would be gorgeous in the night. Your grandmother used to come with me there on every full moon day. I wanted to know whether you would come."

I thought it would be better to go with Nandi than stay alone here. The weather was very chilly. I donned a leather jacket and followed Nandi.

The bank of the Krishna River was stupendous, like a lover, full of deep fondness and shining covertly. Some people were walking together, chanting the names of God. Others were bathing even in that extreme cold, kindling lamps, and leaving them on the water's surface.

After sitting on the riverbank, Nandi asked me if I would go with him on his raft. I also felt like going. So, I said I would.

He took me on the raft to the middle of the river. Devoid of any fear or apprehension, I experienced and cherished a thin light inside me. I felt as if time stopped for a few moments.

After being calm for a brief period, I asked him: "Did my grandmother use to come like this?"

"Yes, *amma*. Lacchuvamma immensely liked to come like this.

"Is it? Have you ever seen an owl?" I asked.

With a thin smile on his face, he replied, "What harm do they do amma? Nothing! At most, they move here and there and keep guarding the people they like. We need not be scared of them."

"I am not scared. I just asked. Have you ever seen a white owl?"

He said, "Aha." He uttered nothing more. I thought he knew something else. I wanted to tell him about my dreams, but didn't say anything. The light of dawn was spreading on the river.

Lacchimi was sobbing. Her father was being taken away. She was surrounded by thick darkness. I wanted to tell her not to weep, but she was not aware of me. Goats were bleating strangely. She drew her limbs in and was lying down. There was no one to take the goats to the hills. I was waking up Lacchimi saying, "Get up, Lacchimi! Let us go to the forest." Lacchimi did not wake up, though I shook her strongly. She didn't even turn to look at me.

Perhaps I woke up with shrieks. My body was drenched in sweat.

"Venamma, Venamma," Nandi was calling me. It seemed he brought milk. I got up.

My neighbours never sit with me and talk. They just smile on seeing me.

Not wanting to stay alone at home one day, I said to Nandi, "I will come with you to the Krishna riverbank," and accompanied him.

He set up a small hut on the riverbank using a kind of reed. When we used to sit there, he would give me boiled peanuts, burned maize seeds or similar things to eat. When he had no major work, he would sit opposite me and weave baskets with bamboo strips. He never even smiled, let alone talked.

My grandmother willed her house and one-acre field to me. She probably knew that I would surely come after her demise. I talked with the tenant farmer and pondered over whom I should give the house to. I had no other work to do here.

I was sure that I would dream that night. I thought that dream wanted to tell me something. I couldn't sleep despite closing my eyes and trying to be calm. I got up and sat on the bed. A few dogs were moaning outside collectively. I opened the window and looked outside. There was no owl. I was deprived of sleep that night. I did not dream but got a fever, maybe due to lack of sleep. Drained, I lay on the bed.

Nandi prepared and gave me some herbal decoction. He also cooked food – broken rice and tamarind pickle. My grandmother would prepare similar food when I had a fever.

"How long have you known my grandmother?" I asked him.

"Your grandmother? Since she was a child!" he said, looking to the other side. Then, he continued, "Have some sleep, Venamma. You need rest. I will go to the riverbank. Boat passengers may have come." He left. I was confused. How could he have known my grandmother since her childhood?

I don't know when I caught forty winks. Lacchimi is moving around me in that same house, with silver rings on her ankles. There were neither hills nor a waterfall. She sat beside me and cradled me in her lap. She placed her cool, soft hand on my forehead and gently fondled my hair. Was this a dream? Was I talking in my sleep? I was not sure of anything.

I woke up in the evening.

I did not dream for the next two days. I felt incomplete and dejected.

In the next dream, Lacchimi caressed me with her hand. She held my hand and took me to a small cave-like place behind the waterfall. She moved a huge boulder aside without any effort. Inside, a man with long shabby braids was sitting on a flat rock, with his eyes closed. Lacchimi bowed in front of him with piety, took water in the pots lying there from a thin stream flowing beside the rock and bathed him with that water. Afterwards, she cleaned his body with a piece of cloth. Then she wrapped a vest around his waist, placed some flowers and fruits before him, and sat facing him. Despite so much activity, he did not move even a bit. Sunrays were coming from some unknown place, touching his dark skin and turning green. His body was full of lustre. After a few moments, he opened his eyes, glanced at Lacchimi and smiled gently. Lacchimi sang a few songs and danced in front of him. I looked at him intently and felt that I had seen him before. Yes, he was Nandi!

I woke up uttering his name. The dream seemed very fresh. Wasn't he Nandi?

That day, when I was rearranging goods in the house, I could not resist my desire to open grandmother's trunk box. I opened it. There were some playthings, a tiny pitcher and two silver rings in it. They were the same rings worn by

Lacchimi in my dreams. There was also a short hand stick that box. It was the same stick held by Lacchimi in my dreams. Were grandmother and Lacchimi the same!?

Nandi didn't come that day. I went searching for him on the riverbank. Nandi wasn't there. Assuming he may have gone to the other bank of the river, I sat there and began to wait for him.

He arrived at high noon. Seeing me in that state, he was distressed. "Venamma, why are you sitting here in this hot sun? Wouldn't I have come in the evening?" he said.

I reminded him of the eleventh day of the funeral rituals the next day. He had some strange power in him that was exhorting me to be with him.

"Nandi, can't you stay with me in the house?" I asked.

He replied, "Am I not staying with you in the evenings? I need to go to the riverbank early in the morning every day."

I wanted to touch him. Wanting to talk with someone is okay, but what could be there behind my desire to touch him? I was at my wits' end. I felt very strongly to touch him at least once. Should I take his permission and touch him, or just stroke as if casually?

No such question arose earlier in my mind.

Nandi left me at the house and departed.

Perhaps I entered a dream by myself. Nobody was there. No Lacchimi, walking in the forest! I went to all the spots which Lacchimi used to frequent. I screamed her name several times. Nowhere could I see her. I went to the waterfall and moved the boulder aside. Nandi was sitting there. Like Lacchimi, I placed flowers and fruits in front of him. His whole body was shining with light. I gave him a fruit.

He said, "I don't eat anything."

I was scared to touch him.

"Are you Nandi?" I asked. He smiled gently.

"How old are you?"

"I have no age."

"Where is Lacchimi? I want her," I wept loudly. "Lacchimi came for you. What have you done to her?" I asked indignantly.

"No, it is I who came for Lacchimi," he said.

I swooned with fury and screamed very loudly.

Water was flowing in the reverse direction in the waterfall. I shrieked so deafeningly that the hills reverberated, and they were floating in the air. He extended his arm and tried to touch my head. At once, the white owl flew towards me, kicked my head, and disappeared.

I woke up with a loud shriek.

I performed all the rituals of the eleventh day. Nandi was beside me and helped me execute them. We mixed grandmother's relics in the Krishna River. I was leaving that village. I didn't know what to talk to Nandi while leaving.

"Will you stay here?" I asked.

"My work is over. I should go," he said.

I felt grieved. I expected him to hold my hand and console me. However, nothing of that sort happened. I wanted to ask him how old he was, but I left without asking that question.

The white owl was flying from the top of the house into the hills.

***

Notes:

Amma: An endearing and revering word for addressing any woman or a child

Frank, the Painter

Someone knocked at my door in the early morning. The way of it indicated that there was something substantial about it. I opened the door a bit eagerly.

It was Nancy. I saw her for the first time in a park.

Frank introduced me to her: "She is a veterinary doctor working nearby. Her name is Shyama. Looking at her, I smiled faintly. She shrank a little and appeared indifferent and observant on that day.

It would be hard to believe that she was the wife of a dynamic person like Frank, for she appeared very ordinary. When I remarked like that any time, Frank would laugh and say that he was practical and sensible because of her.

Frank and I walk regularly in Turtle Park. Our amity strengthened because of it.

In the beginning, he used to tell me not only how his wife loved his paintings, but also how his cat J would sometimes move around his feet. I understood that he had a wife and was raising a cat. As time passed, he talked more about cats and their preferences than about his wife and paintings. Sometimes I felt that he befriended me because I was a vet.

Only after I visited his art exhibition for the first time did I realise he was a celebrity. All his paintings depicted nude women, and almost all showed their backs. After seeing them, I thought of curtailing my visits to him. Frank, however, did not give me that chance. He would talk normally, and I, too, did not want to quit my habit of walking.

Frank is about sixty. He is Italian, and his parents were Americans. "The Italian in me dominates me; I admire beauty more than anything," he would say.

If we said, "The beauty of anything lies in its soul, Frank," he would laugh and continue, "Beauty in soul, heart, body ... these are empty words, Shyama. Beauty is nothing but you finding it beautiful." If we cited the axiom, "Beauty lies in the eyes of the beholder," he would deny it saying, "No. It just depends on the beholder's life, mood and choice."

I saw people buying his paintings for thousands of dollars. The most attracting feature in his paintings lies in the multi-coloured lines that appear to emanate from the nude bodies. We can't make out whether they are being emitted from inside or going in from outside. There is thin light behind those lines. How does he bring out that effect? It is difficult to discern. We feel his brush has life. His paintings don't just make us want to watch them; they express something beyond that. Watching them, many women must have fallen in love with him. I told him the same thing once.

"Painter and painting are two distinct things, Shyama," he said.

"Does it mean there is no painter in a painting?"

"If a painter wants to be a part of a painting, he can never complete it. If he does, he cannot remain an artist."

"What do you see in a model?"

He gave no reply to my question. After a brief pause, however, he said steadily, "Every artist has some secrets. They cannot be explained explicitly. But the artist perceives them in his mind."

This conversation between us pulled me more towards him. Often, I would go to the park just to talk with him. I noticed that he, too, was enjoying my companionship.

Long after I got acquainted with him, I went to his home for the first time. It was an old bungalow with faded walls. Antiquated chairs, a sofa, window curtains, chandeliers ... all were old. Inside, Frank's paintings were visible here and there. I felt he didn't give importance to money. Since then, I started visiting his home frequently. I think I liked the old smell of the building. It seemed Nancy, too, was happy to see me. I thought that not many people came to that house. Perhaps, Frank didn't permit anyone to do so.

Nancy, too, continued her friendship with me. I never saw the cat J that he often referred to. When I asked Nancy about it, she took me to the window of their bedroom. Through it, one could view the distant hills and the tree-filled forest. It is usual to see a forest in that area. However, a fuzzy path appeared to lead to that forest. Nancy told me that occasionally, that cat would come through the window, move around Frank and go back. I was not surprised that Nancy didn't interfere much in Frank's affairs. She told me jocularly that Frank's painting studio was in the basement and nobody except that cat had permission to go there! Though she said it in a lighter vein, I could grasp that Frank and Nancy were not close at all to each other.

Gradually, I met Nancy more frequently than anyone else in that house.

Four months ago, Frank came to our home for the first time without any prior notice. He was silent for a long time. I thought he had come to me to talk about something. "Frank, you can say anything to me. Your secret will be locked safely in my closet," I said, smiling. In fact, I don't usually conceal secrets. Yet, the anxiety in me, thinking he was about to share a secret, prompted me to say that.

"Of late, I feel the power of my seeing and hearing faculties has increased significantly. I can even hear faint sounds very clearly and read very small letters. I don't need spectacles now."

I said, "Isn't it nice? Those faculties usually diminish in old people, but are enhanced in you,"

His eyes appeared strange. There was a perturbation in them, as if looking for something. "I don't know if it is good or bad, but I feel this is not normal I feel," he said.

He sat for some time and then left abruptly. After that, he came to the park less often – at the most, he came once or twice a week. Even then, he looked weary and unstable. I noticed a change in Frank. I enquired about his health and asked him to get all tests done. I gave him some suggestions, too. Frank seemed to listen attentively.

One day, Frank was strolling in front of our gate. Wanting to know what was happening, I called him inside and asked sternly what the matter was. He said he was famished despite eating a lot, couldn't fall asleep even after taking sedative pills and unable to trust anyone. His skin was dry, and his hair had turned red. I pretended not to notice these changes. I asked about his painting work. That, too, seemed to be a problem. He said no models were willing to go to him. When I asked why, he was unwilling to reply.

One day, Nancy came to my house. She said Frank was not sleeping at all; sometimes he went out during the night and howled like a fox. She said she was scared of him. The cat J, too, hadn't been seen lately, she added.

I asked her why models were not willing to come to him. "Even those who used to like him immensely told me that he was behaving strangely. Some said he, too, became naked while painting. Others confessed that they couldn't even bear his touch, and that's why they stopped coming," she said.

After a brief silence, she revealed that she suspected he was turning into some kind of animal.

One evening, I went to his home. The main door opened with just a gentle push. I went in but found neither Frank nor Nancy there. I paced to the basement; I had been waiting for a chance of having a glimpse at Frank's studio for a long time. I smelled paint. I peeked inside cautiously.

Frank was painting a picture, sitting naked. His back was replete with dense, red hair. The light orange-hued painting was partly visible. I saw the half-finished head of some animal. Its eyes were green like Frank's. I was startled, held my breath and returned.

That night, I heard noises as if someone was knocking and scratching on the door. I also heard a faint howl. I looked out through the window. There was a creature, half human and half animal. I could figure it out. I stiffened with extreme fright. All of it happened not in a dream but in reality. I didn't know when I slept amid my fears.

I stopped going to Frank's house.

One morning, Nancy came to my house. She spoke falteringly. "He ran away into the forest," she said. I hugged her.

Had Frank completed the painting of himself?

***

Phantasm

Rarely does that bar look less crowded. People who frequent it as a habit outnumber those who come to mitigate their grief or share their happiness. When we wanted to meet, we would choose that bar. Generally, Sarathi doesn't like to meet anyone or share emotions easily. He rang me after a long gap of time and told me we were to meet there. I knew he would come later than promised, yet I arrived early and started waiting for him.

Sarathi usually looks weary. Today, there is an even more haggard look on his face. Having come with a purpose of talking about something specific, he remained silent for quite some time. I was used to waiting till he opened up on his own. After a little while, he said, "Let us go to your home, Ram." Fortunately, Vasanthi was away from home. We took a whiskey bottle and a snack pack, went home and sat on the balcony of my apartment.

He initiated his protracted conversation saying, "Bidu came after ten years.

"Soon, she said, 'Even if my coming like this and staying with you causes inconvenience to you, it's okay. You can bear a little discomfort for my sake, Sadhu.'

'You know about Bidu. She never laughs aloud or gets enraged. It seems as though she doesn't know that people become furious at times. She is so steadfast. But when Bidu talked with a laugh like that, I felt somewhat odd.

"She spruced herself up a bit, took out a photo of *Sharada Devi* from her bag and placed it on the ledge. That photo had been with her since our college days. She went straight into the kitchen, prepared tea and brought it out. I think she felt nothing new in doing so. When I sipped the basil tea silently, it tasted a little bitter.

'Haven't you married yet?' she asked me suddenly.

"I knew she would ask that question at some time, but never imagined that it would be the very first question.

"Giving a negative reply, I got up saying, 'I will bring some commodities.' She must have understood that I did it to avoid her next question.

'Bring basa fish, banana leaves, and some dried coconut. I will cook a Bengali special for you.'

"As the conversation diverted to food, the atmosphere changed a bit. There was no significant change in her appearance, but her eyes were dry.

"How many days will she stay with me? How did she know my address? Why did she arrive suddenly after so many years? Was she married? If I hadn't been here when she came, maybe she would have gone somewhere else, never to return. She didn't come searching for me. Perhaps because I wanted her to come, she came. If that's true, then if I want her to go, will she go? Will I ever want her to leave me?

“I decided strongly not to ask her anything. However, all those questions hunted and tormented me. I was troubled by them for some time.

“In the evening, when she spoke, her words mingled with the sounds of the passing trains. I thought she was revealing some unknown secrets. I listened to her calmly. In the middle of her talk, she said, ‘I am contemplating staying here.’

“Does it mean that Bidu will stay with me from now on? The very thought of spending nights with her frightened me.

‘Sadhu, thoughts rather than mirth are playing on your face,’ she said, picked some books lying scattered on the shelves and asked, ‘Are you into Buddha now?’

“I smiled with a little annoyance. The thought of spending the night clutched me tightly and didn’t allow me to feel at ease. She rearranged the books on the shelves and cooked food. I didn’t have sufficient courage to ask about her personal matters. I decided not to tell her anything that had happened in the past. Surprisingly, she too, didn’t allude to past incidents.

‘What Sadhu, you’ve been reluctant since I came. Are you thinking that I came here to ask or take anything from you?’

“Her peculiar way of talking, coupled with her smile, highlighted her uniqueness.

‘Nothing of that sort, Bidu,’ I said. I became aware of the uneasiness brewing inside me. Why do people come? Isn’t giving invisible things more difficult than giving visible ones?

"She took a bath, wore white *lalchi* and pyjamas, and sat facing me. Her feet were calloused like those of agricultural women.

'Shall we have lunch?'

'Okay.'

'Today, I will eat from your plate,' she said, like a child.

"Perhaps she noticed the inconvenience on my face. She added, 'Just like that I said. Don't worry. I will eat from a separate plate.' She placed the fish on my plate.

'There are very few bones in this fish. The whole room was filled with a Bengali aroma.

'Fish are called *jalapushpa* in Bengali. Aren't they?'

'Yes, fishes are considered a vegetarian food there.'

"There was a Bengali accent in her Telugu.

'Your father ...' I said, and paused for a moment. I had an apprehension that our conversation might go awry.

"Not giving much attention to my words, she asked me with a smile, 'Your room is beside the rail tracks. Can you sleep?'

'In the beginning, I used to wake up every time when the trains passed. Now, I wake up if they don't come!'

"I placed a bed for her on the floor, a little away from my cot. But she came and sat on my cot.

'I don't sleep anywhere except on a cot. In my childhood, when I slept on the floor, I was bitten by a centipede. Since then, I never sleep on the floor,' she said, and slept beside me.

"I scooted over to the cot's edge and turned my face to the other side. I heard the thumping of my loud heartbeats. I don't know how much time has elapsed. Slowly, she entwined me with her arms from behind. She pressed me hard to her body and began kissing my neck. My prudence melted away slowly. A weakk struggle was defeated in my heart. I turned to the other side and kissed her. Her face was glowing like the moon. I wanted to hug her tightly.

"Astonishingly, her body was not there. My hands touched nothing but fog-like smoke. I didn't understand how she could have hugged me. I opened my eyes abruptly before a shriek could escape my throat. My body was drenched in sweat.

"Bidu was sitting on a chair near the table, writing something. I turned my head and looked at the bed. Nobody was there beside me. She was looking at me, probably because of my shriek.

'What happened, Sadhu? Did you have a dream?'

"The same glow was present on her face. It is difficult to bear such bright light, I thought, and closed my eyes. I could still hear the sound of her movements."

Sarathi stopped his narration.

Bidu was not a stranger to us. We had studied post-graduation together at Andhra University. Though our studies ended ten years ago, Sarathi was still in touch with me. He treats me as a trusted friend. Probably because I am always busy with only my own affairs, or because I don't ask him anything directly or bluntly, I earned his trust.

In our early days at the University, Sarathi's love for Bidu transformed him into a hero. After our final exam, he fled the university one night without telling anyone. Nobody knew what had happened. Bidu made countless inquiries about him and eventually left for Bengal.

When I met him after a few years, I asked him about Bidu first. As he had resorted to binge drinking, I took him to the beach. There, he vomited and screamed terribly. Crying continuously with fright, he said, "Buddy, she is not a human being." I couldn't understand what had frightened him so much.

Later, I happened to meet him in Hyderabad after seven or eight years. There was no change in his appearance. He felt happy seeing me. We used to meet at the bar now and then.

I asked him: "That night you left Bidu. What happened afterwards?"

"That day," Sarathi began hesitantly. "I forced Bidu to stay in my room. At midnight, I drew her close to me and hugged her. When I looked at her while trying to kiss her lips eagerly, I noticed she had no head - only her trunk was there ... and it was naked. I was terrified. I didn't even dare to switch on the light."

"Was it a reality or a dream, Sarathi?"

"I don't know. I felt it was really happening. Even after that, I tried to meet Bidu two or three times. But each time I saw only her trunk. I was very frightened. I didn't know whom to tell about it, so, I fled."

"You didn't see her face then. Are you seeing only her face today?" I asked.

He remained silent for some time.

Then, he mumbled to himself, "I don't understand why this is happening to me. There is nobody who has come so close to me in my life. She used to fill my heart like a tree full of flowers in spring. Unable to bear her, sometimes, I would feel grief. I also felt happy that she could not be banished from my heart, however much I tried. I think she is a goddess who came to punish me. I can neither stay with her nor ask her to leave me."

"Last night you realised fully that it was only a dream. Then why are you afraid of dreams?"

"How do you separate dream from reality? From where and why does fear originate? Can you tell me? Can you draw a line between reality and illusion and say correctly which is which? Perhaps you won't understand all this. It is 2 am now. I will go home," he said and got up.

I did not insist him to stay. I felt he had come to a strong decision.

After that, Sarathi did not call me.

***

Notes:

Lalchi: A type of shirt

Jalapushpa: A Sanskrit expression for fish. Jala means water, pushpa means flower.

Sharada Devi: The Hindu goddess, Saraswathi

Rabeera

I got into the bus. Seeing it, I felt that only the people who want to travel long distances with minimum expenditure, and those who don't give importance to time, would opt for such vehicles. I hoped the seat beside me would remain vacant. Soon, however, he came and sat in the seat next to me. His complexion seemed a mixture of white and pink. The smell coming from him resembled that of green, moist grass. I didn't imagine I would talk to him.

"Where to?" he asked, smiling at me after settling a bit.

It was inevitable for me to reply. His English seemed different, with a kind of slang.

"Up to Little Rock, Arkansas," I replied.

He laughed aloud and said, "That's nice. I will be your company up to your destination."

Strangely, I felt that his laughter resembled that of Rajaiah, the washerman's donkey in our village. I had seen it laugh only once. In my childhood, Rajaiah's donkey was stolen by thieves. But, unable to goad it successfully, they left it along with the stolen heavy goods at the end of the village.

The next morning, Rajaiah found it grazing in an arid patch of land at the village's end.

People used to laugh at Rajaia's donkey, saying it did all kinds of work except that of a donkey. Rajaiah, however, took good care of it. He used to put fewer loads on it and carry the heavy weights himself! The villagers taunted him for his foolishness and made fun of him. Once, Rajaiah came to our house along with his donkey. It seems I asked him whether he was not afraid when the thieves stole his donkey. Though I don't remember the incident fully, the donkey's laughter from that time is still vivid in my memory.

I felt it was wrong on my part to recollect Rajaiah's donkey, upon hearing my co-passenger's laughter. Perhaps I considered donkeys inferior to humans, or that donkeys were animals devoid of emotions.

"Hello, Miss, do you need any water?" he asked me. I took the bottle from him, and darted a look to indicate my gratitude.

Without doffing his hat, the cowboy said, "My name is Henny."

"My name is May," I replied. My mouth didn't cooperate with me to reveal my full name. Perhaps some inner defence mechanism works that way.

"Your name is very interesting. Your parents named you after a month, which means you are a very prominent person." He laughed loudly. I reciprocated with a smile as a response to his silly joke. He didn't pay much attention to my smile.

The bus started. He placed his cowboy hat on his face and fell asleep. I had never seen anyone fall asleep so quickly. There was a red string on his wrist. I looked at it inquisitively. It had big white beads in the middle, and two copper coins were tied to it as well.

I reminisced about Sethu.

This journey was meant only to escape from him. We see tormentors and abusers everywhere, but people like Sethu are rare. They insidiously occupy others' lives like slow poison, rendering them helpless and dependent. To live with such people is equivalent to staying beside a canal filled with toxic effluents and breathing the air that comes from it.

Moreover, Sethu claims that all of it is only for my sake.

Sethu and I work for the same company. At first, he was my friend. Later, gradually, he was trying to take a place in my life. I thought I must wake up at least now. I changed my job without letting him know about it. I told him that I was going to a far-off place and asked him not to try to meet me. Then, I left the company.

That is a dream – a dream I experienced. Dreams keep coming again and again, but we cannot go with them.

Sethu must be telling everyone there that I am a selfish person.

Nobody knows who is selfish and to what extent. In fact, nobody wants that. As long as you don't point out others' selfishness, you are considered a nice and great selfless person.

Should you point out, they expose you selfish nature while concealing their own selfishness.

Sethu! Whatever it is, you stay safe. Forgive me if I could not be of help to you. If you choose another person, make a sketch honestly. Someone will easily shower love on you if you lament.

Swinging in the smoothly speeding bus, I felt sleepy.

The driver applied the brakes all of a sudden. Henny caught hold of my hand tightly. I staggered and stood up immediately. Henny didn't let go of my hand; instead, he held it more firmly. I tried to let it go, but to no avail. Then, I noticed that his hand was warm. His eyes were closed, and his hands were trembling. I think he held my hand for support.

"Henny, are you okay?" I asked.

He opened his eyes. Seeing my hand in his hand, he felt relieved and laughed. Placing his other hand on mine, he remarked: "There is some healing power in your hand, May. It reduced the pace of my heartbeats."

I thought he was flirting. His glances, however, indicated otherwise. I hadn't known him until just two hours ago, but I trust him now.

Pointing at the red string on his wrist, I asked, "What is this?"

"It is a sign of Rabeera."

"Rabeera! Who is Rabeera?"

"Rabeera is a donkey."

I was startled. Rajaiah's donkey, which had come to my mind a little while ago, moved in front of my eyes.

"I was born and brought up in Idaho. There, my father brought a donkey for me. Everyone laughed, saying, 'Your father gave you a donkey as a gift.' Gradually, Rabeera and I became close friends." He paused, then added glancing at me, "May, I am saying something, but you seem immersed in your own thoughts."

"No, Henny! Please proceed," I said, trying to conceal my surprise.

"Rabeera used to talk to me and look after me. Once, I went to the hills with my friends, and got lost. Not knowing the way to my home, I stayed in the hills that night. Everyone began searching for me. At last, Rabeera came looking for me and took me home."

"Do donkeys have such intuition?"

"Otherwise, it wouldn't come and spotted me there." He went on, telling me many things, such as donkeys don't shed tears, donkeys sleep standing up, and so on.

I thought he wouldn't stop talking about donkeys even if I tried to stop him. Interrupting his continuous talk, I said laughingly, "So, you say donkeys are better than humans."

He appeared to have been hurt. "How can we compare Rabeera with humans?" he said with a serious face.

I felt like taunting him a little, so I said, "When I saw your laughter, I thought it was like that of a donkey in my native village."

"Hey! Have you seen a donkey laugh? May you are not a normal girl. Donkeys never reveal their emotions except on certain special occasions, and that too in the company of trusted persons. But, it is not very strange if a donkey laughs near you," he said thoughtfully.

It seemed he didn't pay much heed to my words. I was amused by his response and felt like laughing.

"Why?" I asked.

He said with a smile, "You reminded me of Hygea. My grandmother used to tell repeatedly that my ancestors came from Rome. Often, she would talk about Hygea. She had a book with pictures of Greek gods in it. You look like a goddess called Hygea in that book."

This time, there was a slight glint in his smile.

This fellow is comparing me to a goddess. I should tell him about Sethu, who is publicising that I am a demon full of venom.

"Who is she?"

He said, "She is the goddess of health. I saw two pictures of her in that book: in one, she is sitting, wearing the long gown of Virgin Mary, and feeding a snake. In the other, she is leaning towards her father and smiling." Then, he switched back to talking about Rabeera.

This time, I kept my hand in my lap.

After a little while, he took out a few plums from his bag and gave one to me. I assumed it would be sore, but it was very sweet. Its taste took me to some plum trees on distant hills.

"I never ate such sweet plums before," I said in amazement.

"Perhaps you've never consumed the fruits of a real plum tree, May."

My stomach was full, but I didn't understand what he meant by real tree.

"How is Rabeera now?"

"I left Rabeera in the hills long ago. It didn't like to come into the midst of humans."

"You are a hill dweller."

"Yes, I am," he said and went on recounting stories about the surrounding hills, trees, and Rabeera. Intermittently, he talked about his grandmother and the dishes she used to cook.

His words were like a mountain breeze. Abruptly, I felt affection and love for him. It seems I had now gotten used to the smell of green grass emanating from him. This time, I sat relaxed, leaning against his shoulder. Though I had been travelling with him for just four hours, I now liked him. How did affection result so easily!?

Before the next stop came, a hubbub ensued, and the bus slowed down.

"It looks like we are approaching Dallas. We have a transit time of one hour. We need to change buses here, I suppose," I said.

I wanted to talk with him some more.

“I will get down in Dallas.”

Why? Didn’t you say you were going up to Little Rock?”

“I have my pickup truck in Dallas. I will go in it.”

For a moment, I thought he was lying to me. I suspected that he was getting down in Dallas intentionally. Why did he sit beside me? I repented for having travelled with him.

I scooted over a little and leaned against the window.

He is a donkey man, I thought. I laughed, but didn’t like the way I satisfied my ego. Even if he had continued to travel with me, he would have stayed only a few more hours. Wouldn’t he?

Sethu, and Henny are normal people. However, there is a difference only in the time they travelled with me.

Half of my journey is over. I have to change buses here. I need to complete my journey by sleeping or looking out from the window. I had company for just half of my travel time. I can sleep peacefully if the seat beside me remains vacant. The bus reached Dallas station.

It appeared that the bus sighed heavily. Perhaps it could not understand me!

***

Bonjour

A ten-year-old boy with dimpled cheeks was coming towards me with a smile. When I turned back to have a glimpse of my co-tourists, they had already dispersed. It was a small village in the Alps Mountains, and the boy looked as though he knew everything there. Standing in front of me, he said, "Come this way."

I glanced at my watch. I had one hour and realised there was enough time for me to join the tourism bus. I thought they employed such children to attract customers. Perhaps the same happens in every country. But here I felt as though I had come into the Stone Age. With gigantic boulders on either side, streets were slightly narrow. Not many people were seen around. In the morning, the guide, Richo joked: "In this winter time, no one except artists and beautiful people come here." His English, spoken with a French accent, was charming. So was his way of pronouncing the word Bonjour. Richo looked into my eyes while explaining anything to us, as if he was speaking only to me. These French men, perhaps, divulge their liking for women openly.

The dimple-cheeked boy was pacing exuberantly. When I saw his shabby leather jacket and woollen cap, I was reminded of the shepherd Damu in our village. Damu was always seen wearing his father's old coat and a cloth cap. When asked why he was absent from school, he would say that Lacchimi gave birth to a baby goat or Raju was injured, and so on. He gave names to all his goats. When asked why had done so, he would reply, "I don't understand goats' language, so their names are not known to me. Each goat must be having a name in their own language. So how can I call 'O goat'! That's why I gave a name to each goat." A peculiar smell of goats used to emanate from him.

He led me to a homestead that looked like a shop and stopped there. Wind chimes were dangling in front of that house; the small wooden house amid bamboo sticks swayed a little when the wind blew. A thin whistle-like sound was heard, probably because of the wind passing through the bamboo sticks. It was like a song born in the forest. Glancing at me with smiling eyes, he gestured me to go inside. A fragrance of lavender seemed to have slowly encircled me. On one side, there were bunches of dried lavender flowers, small perfume bottles, and scarves made of silk and wool. I saw a woman in a chair beside the counter and tried to figure out her age. She must be old, I thought. She was knitting a scarf. She raised her eyelids and looked at me. A small lightning-like spark flashed in her eyes. Even ordinary people would become artists on these mountains, I thought.

She spoke to me in clear English: "My name is Elera. I am glad you have come here." Smiling, I looked at her. She gazed at me intently without batting her eyelids for some time. I felt she was searching for something in me.

"Do you want to buy anything here? Have you liked anything?" she asked.

I gestured at the dried lavender flowers. She took out some lavender flowers that were kept in a blue cover. "These are true French lavenders. Take these," she said.

"What is their price?" I asked.

"It's all right. I don't want to take money from you."

I wanted to ask the reason for this, but queerly, I nodded my head lightly without insisting.

"You have come from India, haven't you? Your strong Indian accent is revealing it. When I see any Indian with a complexion like yours, I am reminded of my friend Shyama. I studied in India for a brief period," she said.

With the mention of India, interest welled up in me. She was at least seventy years old.

With a bit of curiosity, I asked, "Where did you study?"

"At Shanthinikethan!"

I looked at her once more, inquiringly. She had blue eyes, pale, wrinkled skin and coppery hair. Some kind of light seemed to emanate from her. I was amused at my own misconception.

"Then, you know Tagore's *Geetanjali*. Don't you?"

Suddenly, her face blossomed like a hibiscus flower. She went behind the desk and took out a crinkled book. It was Geethanjali.

"It is this book that has been making me love the world," she said.

I knew France is the home of artists. They value art immensely.

"Have you read it?" she asked.

I said, "Yes. What else is beautiful here?"

"There are some things that are at a place a bit far away. If you have time, I will show them to you," she said. I looked at my watch and wanted to decline, but I could not do so.

"You are like a June flower. I will call you June," she said without bothering to know my actual name. I was startled. One day, Damu brought a baby goat and asked me to give it a name. I gave the name June. His smiling face beamed.

"Will you come with me, June? I want to spend this daytime with you."

I, too, felt like spending time with Elera. Notwithstanding vacillation, I couldn't say no to her. Reminded of joining the group, I looked at my watch.

Elera laughed and said, "Why are you looking at your watch? Don't worry. Time won't go anywhere until it forces us to move. I have been thinking that a friend would arrive, and you have come." There was a smile in her eyes.

The dimple-cheeked boy who brought me was gone. I asked her, "Who is the boy that brought me here?"

"His name is Cherub. He knows well whom to bring here. Before you leave, there is a precondition for you," said she.

"What is that?" I asked with perplexity in my mind.

"You should forget yesterday and tomorrow as long as you are with me. Also, have no questions."

Is stopping a question possible?

We started in her small pickup truck. I could make out that the vehicle was entering a valley. The path had slopes. Elera drove the vehicle very slowly. With mountains around, the place looked safe. After some time, we halted in front of Elera's house. It was situated at some height at the centre of a mountain. It was a small house with flat ground in the front. As if inviting people, it emitted a kind of pleasantness. Maybe people are needed for cheerfulness. At first, I sat on a rock pial without going inside. A faint fragrance of lavenders was felt. Elera came with tea in small cups. While drinking that tea, I experienced the comeliness of lavender gardens. The sun was about to set. With Geetanjali in her hand, Elera started reading it.

The time that my journey takes is long and the way of it long.

I came out on the chariot of the first gleam of light, and pursued my voyage through the wilderness of the world, leaving my track on many a star and planet.

It is the most distant course that comes nearest to thyself, and that training is the most intricate which leads to the utter simplicity of a tune.

The traveller has to knock at every alien door to come to his own, and one has to wander through all the outer worlds to reach the innermost shrine at the end.

My eyes strayed far and wide before I shut them and said, "Here art though!"

The question and the cry "Oh, where?" melt into tears of a thousand streams and deluge the world with the flood of the assurance "I am!"

My eyes moistened. The scent of Geetanjali pervaded the area. The soaring vehemence and all the fears cooled down. The inner river, its flow as well as the running time, slowed down. A light drizzle started. Raindrops enveloped me passionately.

"It's drizzling. The wind turned chilly, too. Shall we go in?"

I entered the house. I experienced a déjà vu feeling. The place looked quite familiar to me, and I thought I had lived there once. Elera was humming a tune and working simultaneously. It was warm inside with a burning fireplace. There was thin light around the firewood as though it was the same light that surrounded Elera. A sweet smell of bread was coming from the oven. Pouring olive oil from a small utensil, she was cooking soup with small fish. "These are called anchovies. I hope you eat fish," she said.

I was watching her without moving. There were tiny paintings on the walls. Thin darkness spread out. The silence was charming.

But why am I scared when he works silently? His emotionless look did not exhibit any tedium. Unable to tolerate his touch replete with inordinate love and affection, I escaped from him! He said, "You always want people. You are a vast emptiness inside though. There is nothing except blankness in you," and left me. He who had given his verdict that I had no love inside me – can he bear this silence?

Elera called me: "June, we don't have much time. Come here." I recollected Elera's precondition.

I had never tasted such a delicious dish before. I had no thoughts in my mind.

Except for reading Geetanjali and uttering a few words, nothing more had taken place.

The rain intensified. It appeared as though snow was falling, too. Because of the fireplace, the chill was not felt much. I lay down cosily on a small cot. Elera came and sat beside me. She laid in my neck the wreath that she had woven with light blue roses. I didn't know when she had completed weaving it. "Good night, my child," she said and kissed lightly on my forehead. Sleep overcame me. I was reminded of the love in Damu's eyes when he stole goat milk and brought it for me.

Richo was saying to a newly-wedded couple in front of me in English with a French accent: "In this winter season, nobody except artists and beautiful people would visit places like this." Where was I? What is all this? Is it true that there is no Elera around? I was, however, feeling the scarf around my neck, and the scent of lavenders. Hasn't all this happened at all?

All the couples were reciting "Bonjour, Lakshmi!" I was still in bewilderment. After a long time, snow rained heavily last night. "How would it be there?" Richo was saying. Some said we should go, while others argued against it. As I insisted that we should go, all agreed and started. I felt that the journey was not new to me; I understood I had seen it before. When we reached there, we were told that everything was shut due to the cold. Therefore, we had to return. Even in that severe chill, I wanted to go and see Elera's shop.

We understood that the big gate was closed. I got down and walked a little ahead. Then, I saw the dimple-cheeked boy, Cherub. He was coming to me with a smile. There were scarves in his hands. He was asking me to buy the woollen scarf with light blue and rose colours. A faint whistle entered the bamboos saying "Bonjour."

Pari, Alias Parvathi

"There is still some time before Satyam arrives."

"It's all right. I need to know the truth," I said to Murthy.

"For how many more days will you continue your investigation? And what is the use of it? He has done something nasty, I agree. But can't you leave the issue, Paree?"

I could sense the change in Murthy's tone.

"Murthy, listen to me. If people who are never just and always very selfish are willing to help us in a big way, it means one day they will deceive us equally big," I said decisively.

"Why do you have so much distrust for him? Your attitude has been the same from the beginning!" said Murthy.

My eyes became teary upon hearing his words.

"Frankly speaking, you and he are not fundamentally different. Only your pursuits and motives are different. There is adamancy in both of you. You say he is selfish, but your selflessness is, in a way kind of selfishness," said Murthy.

I know I cannot argue with Murthy. He is the only close friend that Satyam and I have. If I press for any help, Murthy would oblige even at the cost of his life. He is working as a political reporter in a popular newspaper. He knows well what motives people have behind their work and how they should be regarded. It seems he noticed the stiffening of my jaw.

"So, do you insist that we should go?" Murthy said, realising that it was inevitable.

We set out early at five in the morning. Murthy was mum. Didn't he like my going there, or is there any other reason for his silence? I couldn't understand. After appearing pensive for a long time, he asked, "Even if you discover something after going there, what will you do?" His question revealed his peevishness rather than his desire to know my answer.

"I don't know."

"Whatever ... he is not as bad as you think."

"How bad did I think of him? Do you know?" I asked directly.

"..."

"But, I want to say one thing, Murthy. If uprightness is seen in unexpected circumstances, we get many doubts about its veracity. No problem if Satyam is selfish. However, if he is upright on some pretext, it is tantamount to something worse than selfishness. Then, I have to forgo all hopes in him."

I thought he would ask what hopes they are. But he didn't ask. I could perceive his protest behind his calmness. Murthy stopped the car on the way and brought tea. We both had it. Murthy retained all my likes and dislikes in his mind, which made me proud. He became a bit more normal now. It was a four-hour-journey. We reached Erragondapalem. The road was very bumpy beyond that village. The car was tossing.

"What will be the condition of your car at the end of this journey? Anyhow, it is time you changed your car," I said, and continued, "Murthy, what do you think of me for my crazy desires?"

His eyes shrank and gleamed a little.

Lot of dust was rising behind the car. There were not many trees along the road. Big boulders appeared here and there, though. I thought we had entered a desert. The sunshine was scorching. Ten to twelve kilometres went by that way. Murthy veered his car a little. A small mud house came into view. We opened its small gate and entered. The door was closed, and nobody was there. Murthy went out and enquired with the neighbours where Parvathamma had gone. They told that she had gone to her field.

Is this Parvathamma's house? Satyam helped her a lot. Then why the house is so desolate?

Murthy asked, "Shall we go to the field?"

We drove in the car till the end of the mud path and went on foot from there. I walked with Murthy, listening to his words. Some crops looked dried up, while others appeared green. A person's image was seen moving amidst green maize corns. Murthy yelled, "Sambaiah!" He came out slowly, walking from inside the crop. He was small, with a cloth wound around his head. "You thought of the village after a long gap," said he. Murthy enquired about Parvathamma.

"She is at the well," Sambaiah pointed his hand in that direction. A well could be seen there. A small snake slithered by me as I walked along a ridge. I jumped off to the other side. Not bothering about it, Murthy paced ahead. However, I was startled.

Parvathamma looked thin and tiny. The silver rings on her legs attracted my attention first. I vaguely recalled seeing them in my childhood. After that, I saw her again once when my father passed away. My mother asked her to stay with us. She, however, declined, saying, "No *amma*, I can't stay." She went back.

She had aged. She tucked her sari hem a bit high. There was a wide rock with a sickle beside it. Sighting Murthy, she greeted him, "It has been a long time, Murthayya." Her voice sounded special.

"Were you scared seeing a snake? You resemble Satthem a lot," she said.

Looking at me and Murthy, she asked, "Is Satthem okay?" We kept quiet.

Parvathamma shouted, "*Orey* Samba, bring maize cobs and green gram pods. They are at the far end of the field." Turning to us, she asked us to sit. We understood that we had to sit on the ground. It was a small problem for me. She burned the maize cobs over a thin fire and gave them to us. Beside the well, there was a banyan tree. Many prop roots hung from it. We ate maize and green gram in the cool shade of the tree and relished them. Parvathamma did not talk much.

The sun had set. The surroundings cooled down a bit. Egrets were flying in the sky in groups. They looked like strings of pearls. Parvathamma said, "Lacchuvamma's group has left for home. Lassie, have you made the sun set early? Let us go."

I could surmise that she was referring to the flock of egrets as Lacchuvamma's group. I forgot the questions that I wanted to ask her. After reaching home, Parvathamma asked us to take a bath, laid cots in the front yard and covered them with sheets. It seemed that bathrooms were built recently at the back of the house. By the time we freshened up, she had made maize rotis and a curry. Murthy had escaped to somewhere, it seemed. She asked about him. I told her he went to drop someone off in the town and would return soon.

I asked her, "Does Satyam come here often?" She gave no reply.

I could faintly recollect the appearance of Parvathamma, who worked in our home during my childhood. She would walk around with her silver anklets. Perhaps I was six then. Once, when I returned from home after summer vacation, she was not there. I recalled my grandmother, who would not come out from her room often. She always used to be somewhat sad or think of God. My grandmother never addressed me, nor did she draw me near her. My father used to attend to all her needs. She did not even talk much to my father. However, she showered inordinate love on Satyam and pampered him excessively. She never doted on anybody so much, though. My mother used to remark that Satyam became highly selfish only because of her extreme fondness.

Grandmother did not live long after that. Perhaps I was ten when she passed away.

"Don't you have anybody?"

"I had an elder brother. He took countless loans from the villagers, mortgaged our field, and fled. I was damn distraught. When we informed your mother of the events, she sent Satthem. He paid all the debts and redeemed our field," said Parvathamma. Her voice betrayed no emotions.

"Does Satyam keep coming here?"

This time too, she did not give any answer.

"You used to work in our home. Why did you leave?"

"Your grandmother accused me of developing much attachment to Satyam, and asked me to leave."

"When did you come to our home for the first time?"

"When your grandfather married your grandmother and brought her here, I accompanied her. As my father could not repay the loan taken from your grandfather, I was left to your grandfather."

"Didn't you go back to your home even once?" My voice sounded feeble to myself.

"Your grandmother hadn't begotten children. So, I had to remain here."

That means ....

Murthy did not come. Parvathamma and I lay side by side on cots in the front yard. Stars were twinkling above, but there was no moon in the sky. She started humming *Bhaja Govindam* in undertone. I had listened to it in my father's voice umpteen times. He would sing it to make us sleep. However, he never went to any temple nor did he bow to God. So, it used to seem very weird to me.

"Do you stay alone here?"

"Why alone? There is a river nearby. There are crops and people around. When did I stay alone?" Her eyes were gazing plainly at the sky.

I wanted to ask her to come with me, but the proposition seemed heavy.

Parvathamma got up, took water from a pot, and drank it. I looked at her with a fixed gaze. I saw my father's mien in her. Mainly, the way she drank water was specific. Her fingers, eyes, thin lips, gait, and way of talking ... everything betrayed my father's resemblance. I was startled. Not wanting to reflect further, I closed my eyes. I didn't know when her Bhaja Govindam song made me sleep.

"We see people like Parvathamma very rarely. She is a bumpkin. Because she is natural like earth, I come here now and then ..." said Murthy in the car while going back.

"... It seems she is a person very close to you." There was a glint of smile on his face.

"What did you gain from the visit? What could you appraise?."

"Murthy, I think we should not try to understand a few incidents too completely and too deeply. Maybe we should let them pass."

In my childhood, Satyam used to shake trees immediately after rain, make water drops fall on me, laugh mischievously, and run away. He came to my mind.

***

Notes:

Amma: An endearing term used for accosting women in India

Orey: Hey

Bhaja Govindam: A popular Hindu devotional poem in Sanskrit composed by Adi Shankaracharya

Eureka

"There used to live some families on the bank of the Orange River in South Africa. Jacob's family was one of them. When Jacob was playing with his sister near the river, he saw a small stone sparkling with tinges of blue and white. Though covered partly by mud, it was dazzling. Jacob took it and washed it thoroughly. As it had an unusual lustre, he gave it to his sister, hoping she would enjoy playing with it. Their mother gave it to the neighbours and requested them to examine it. Thus, it reached people who collect coloured stones. At last, it was discovered to be a valuable diamond. They named it Eureka.

"Since then, hundreds of people and firms started visiting the bank of the Orange River. They went on mining the soil for diamonds. As a result, a deepest manmade mineshaft formed in that area and countless diamonds were mined. Did Jacob reflect on why Eureka was discovered?" Muju would pose a question in the middle of her story and push me into a quandary.

"If not Jacob, someone else would have spotted it. However, he might not have pondered in that way. Ultimately, what happened to Jacob?"

"His family left the area after some time."

Often, I used to feel bored to listen to Muju's stories. Sometimes, I would become peevish too. Unable to control it, I used to get irritated now and then. Yet, the low-pitched huskiness in her voice and the connection it had with life would not let me avoid listening to them.

She used to commence with, "Suri, you must listen to this story carefully, for I may not remember it later." Many a time, I would not understand for quite some days why she had related a particular story.

Muju used to explain about her name somewhat strangely:

"Muju is the name of a Buddhist monk. It implies garbage. I was told that my mother was astonished at people giving such a name to children. After my birth, our family went totally bankrupt and had no shelter, even. Ours was a large family, but it was shattered, and they migrated to different areas. They thought I was the sole reason for all this and contemplated selling me to someone. My grandfather resisted it, adopted me and reared me. But he too landed in difficulties after my going there. In the end, he married me off to your father and died. Before passing away, he beseeched: 'Muju is very special for me. Don't change her name.'"

I was about nine years old when Muju came to our home. Immediately after arriving, she took my sister, Seni, in her arms and kissed her. Since then, Seni would never leave Muju even for a moment and always rambled behind her. Soon after marrying Muju, my father became a drunkard, fell into a gutter and turned bedridden. As there was nobody to give him money for drinking, he would divert all his fury onto Muju. My grandmother used to always berate Muju, saying, 'My son became bedridden only after you entered our home.' However much people reproached and troubled her, Muju's face would never betray any emotion. She appeared very shrewd when alone. However, she used to get admonished in front of others, like a stupid woman. I could not understand why she behaved like that.

Muju brought a trunk box too when she came to our house. One day, I ransacked it when she was not around. I found a silver coin wrapped in papers. I took and stowed it for myself.

One day, she gave me rice mixed with buttermilk and excessive chilli powder. When I was screaming due to the spiciness, she poured sugar in my mouth and began telling a story for the first time. Later, I stealthily put the silver coin in her box.

From that day, we became close friends.

Muju used to laugh very rarely. But when she did, she would continue to laugh for hours. There was something more than cruelty in her laughter. Nobody, including my grandmother, would venture to go near her on such occasions. It was my grandmother's strong belief that something sinister would occur every time Muju laughed. Once, a beam broke and dropped down; another time, my grandfather went mad and fled home. Such incidents were discussed queerly, not just in our home but also in the town.

Like always, one day, she prepared maize porridge and gave it to my father. The porcelain bowl, in which the porridge was served, fell from his hand and shattered. Enraged, my father raised his hand to beat Muju. To everyone's astonishment, my father jumped two feet high into the air and fell down. None of us could comprehend what had happened. Meanwhile, my grandmother came down heavily on Muju, took a stout stick in her hand and rushed towards her.

Muju started to howl. Scared, my grandmother scurried away, ranting. Muju's laughter gradually intensified. My father got a fever. My grandmother was not to be seen; we didn't know where she had hidden. Seni and I sat under the tree in front of our house. The entire street reverberated with Muju's guffaws. Unable to hear it, all our neighbours shut their windows and remained inside their houses. The whole street became deserted. Muju laughed incessantly for five hours. Silence and scare prevailed in our house throughout the day.

In the evening, Muju took Seni and went to the riverbank, and I followed them. Muju sat there until night, hurling stones into the river. I observed them from a distance. Seni, too, played with her, flinging stones into the river. Finally, she pushed a boulder into the water and got up. It went to some distance in the water and stopped. She returned home and had her supper.

Everyone heaved a sigh of relief as nothing bad happened.

That day, I could not sleep until late night. I thought Muju would leave our house. Just that thought engendered much grief in me. My father and grandmother could not live if Muju left our house. They only knew how to hold Muju responsible for anything that occurred. If Muju left, it would be very difficult for me to stay with grandmother, who is a termagant, and father, who always lies on the cot, pestering for alcohol.

I got up and glanced at Muju. She and Seni were sleeping on the bed. I went outside for some time, came back and went to bed.

I pondered where Muju would go. She had neither my grandfather nor any other person. She didn't seem to talk to anybody. Long ago, she told me that she liked the forest in the hills. Maybe she would go there.

Muju left her box, held Seni's hand and set out. She got some diamond, so she will not stay with us anymore. I wanted to tell her that I also wanted to join them. I didn't need to tell her anything particularly, for she always knows my thoughts. I thought she would take me with her.

I started to walk behind them. She headed towards the forest. As the forest came nearer, she began to run. Seni and I were behind her. Once we entered the forest, Muju turned into a bear. I couldn't believe my own eyes. Gradually, our bodies, too, began to change. Our legs and calf muscles became strong. Dense hair started growing on our bodies. We were running faster on four legs.

Muju's laughter echoed throughout the forest.

***

Sea and Ross

Hasn't all this really happened? Then why is this world saying so? I never imagined that such a person would come. I looked at my wrist; the string of coloured beads was hugging my wrist as if naturally.

*

We were carefully listening to his words. We called him Captain. I presume he had been introduced to us just fifteen minutes ago. He sat with us and was talking.

Somehow, I felt that he was a bit highly strung. He was attractive; he threw his eyes up funnily and made us respond positively. It seemed as if he was talking through his nose. Perhaps this was the first time I liked a man's appearance so immensely. His gaunt loin may not have been the reason for it. t could have been his nose or his Spanish accent. He said, "Some people who were supposed to come have not arrived. Can I sit with you for some time?" and sat very close to us. We, who had been talking among ourselves in low voices until then, looked at the new man keenly.

"Have you listened to the sea's sound? We feel as though the sea is talking to us. But if we go into its middle, we realise it is very calm. As its depth increases, its sound decreases." Someone among us remarked, "It seems you know a great deal about the sea." He said that he had worked as a ship's captain for a long time. We decided to call him Captain. He appeared to be looking at me with special attention. I felt a little proud in my mind.

He began to narrate stories about the sea fervently. He described his adventures in the Bermuda Triangle. Saying that gravitational force is formidable there and it would pull us if we went near, he hurled a smile at me, funnily. Sensing that his sentences were directed at me, I felt amused in my heart. He described how he had tactfully salvaged a ship and remarked that the sea and he were mutual friends. He said the sea became his friend many births ago, and the same feeling burgeons in one's heart when one sees certain people. Probably they are the ones whom we had loved long ago, he added. He asked me probingly what my opinion about it was. I replied that I don't believe such things and dismissed them as absurd explanations for the attraction between members of the opposite sex. It seemed that besides me, my co-tourists were enjoying his conversation.

I didn't believe that all he was saying was true, but his method of description was enchanting. He reminded me of Johnny Depp in the movie Pirates of the Caribbean. There is always something likeable in everybody; he may be a big liar, swindler or a drunkard. Some goodness or an indeclinable allurement! There is something similar in this Captain, I thought. He was describing the moonrise at midnight in the midst of the sea, and depicting the feeling of romance on such occasions. As I felt that the conversation was going awry, I stopped looking at him.

Changing the topic, I asked him which region he belonged to and which place he hailed from. That was my first question after listening to him for a long time.

He said, "I was reflecting on why you haven't asked it yet. Tell me, amigos, how does it matter? Aren't we together now? And isn't that more important?" All laughed and nodded their heads. He continued, "Yet, the girl with elongated eyes had asked the question. So, I must answer her. If I want to tell about myself, I have to begin from my grandfather." All said, "Oh," and released a sigh. He resumed his talk: "Contrary to what you presume, mine is not a history of landlords. You will understand better if I recount it from there. Shall I?" he glanced at me. I moved a bit forward.

"My forefathers used to live in the Channel Islands in the Pacific Ocean. Sea lions used to come there. They would arrive on the sea sand during the mating season. Once, a sea lion died after giving birth to a baby whose father had gone into the ocean and never returned. My father gave it the name Ross and reared it. My mother was brought up along with Ross. Ross used to love my mother enormously.

"Ross would never leave my mother. My grandfather and Ross used to go into the sea for hunting. My mother loved a merchant who used to cruise on ships for business purposes. He went into the sea and never returned. On certain special occasions, my grandfather, Ross, my mother and I would go into sea on a boat. Once, when we were caught in a raging storm, our boat sank. Ross rescued my grandfather and me and went into the sea in search of my mother. My grandfather used to tell me that Ross would come to the seashore on and off, sing a quaint song, and go back. People in my village used to say that my grandfather had come from caves inside the sea, and that is why he became a friend of Ross. That way, I belong to the caves of the sea," he said, beaming.

All appeared to be listening to him attentively. Suddenly, he started singing a song. It was a peculiar one. English and Spanish words were mingled in it. He whistled intermittently. The song ran thus:

Moon took the sea into its fold

The moonlight is touching me.

My heart is losing control

And reaching my beloved

Searching for her lap

My eyes are filled with beauty now

Her hair is calling me

O sea! Permit me to go

Let me join her

He was looking into the sky, laughing and singing. His voice seemed to shower slight intoxication. He came and sat beside me on the pretext of stoking the fire. It was then that I noticed a string of coloured beads tied on his wrist. There was also a small, conch-shaped tattoo. His hands were strong, and his fingers were thin and long like those of an artist. He gently laid his hand on mine and left. I did not understand its meaning.

The song halted.

I asked him, 'Do you meet strangers like this on the seashore?'

'Not strangers but those whom I ought to meet. Else, they would never meet me. Those, whom I don't need to meet, do not remember me or my stories. Didn't I tell you that I am a man from the caves of the sea?'

He appeared like a magician. He asked me where I hailed from. He was moving near me. A faint smell of orange came from him.

Unlike you, I was born on the earth, not in a cave of the sea, I said tauntingly.

He smiled and said, 'It doesn't seem like that to me. You must have dropped to the earth from the sky.'

'How should I call you?' He said. 'You tell,' I replied.

He said, 'You are a novia, which means a lover.' He laughed. 'Your smile is pure, your heart is softer than cotton,' he said.

Suddenly, he removed the string of coloured beads from his wrist and tied it on mine. He whispered in my ear, saying that I was lighter than air. His lips touched the tips of my ear. I felt for a few moments as if time was frozen. I thought I was close to him only during that brief period. I liked his comment that I was his lover lost long ago. He was the lover, I guessed.

I recognised him. I have been waiting for him. He knew that my body was very light and my heart was akin to a cloud.

A light drizzle started, followed immediately by lightning and thunder. We all got up and scrambled towards our cottages.

I woke up late. I Ross would come to the seashore on and off, sing a quaint song, and go back. The captain came to my mind. I enquired with my co-travellers about him. Ross would come to the seashore on and off, sing a quaint song, and go back. It hadn't rained the previous night, they averred. I ran to the place where we lit fire. Nothing was seen there.

Is this just a dream? I wondered. I could still feel his orange scent. I saw some signs of sea lion in the sand there. I kept looking at the sea. I felt that I understood a little and yet did not understand anything. The sea understood something. As if telling me something, the waves touched me and retreated. Was he the same Ross whom he had described? Why did he come to the seashore? Was it for me? Did he see the sea and the sea lion in me? I returned, staring at the string of coloured beads on my wrist.

***

She – Dasu

When did this fear actually start? Shanta is asking me. She did a Ph. D. in psychology. I can never forget some experiences; they turn into apprehensions and haunt us. I dismissed a hundred times the incident that occurred in Nagalakshmi Madam's house as a mere imagination. Yet, it is an unforgettable night.

I often used to visit Nagalakshmi Madam's house. I have a special liking for her. She is a friend of my aunt. My visits to Madam's house increased mainly after my aunt had left for Australia. For everything, from a small piece of advice to ideology, I used to talk with her. She would not speak much but would listen to me and ask questions in between. There was never any discussion about whether I answered all her questions and, if I did, they were correct. I liked the ginger tea she gave me whenever I visited her. When I inhaled the aroma of her tea, I felt as if she mixed some unknown magic in it. Her house was always tidy and well-organised, with mud dolls, multi-coloured pillows, light blue curtains and so on. She liked all of them.

I need to talk about her plants in detail. One would wonder if she had grown a forest around her house. Though there wasn't much land around her house, she grew many flower plants and fruit trees in whatever ground was available. While walking amongst the plants, she would look like a goddess of greenery and used to be very vivacious. She would say that plants talk, have a heart, and there is no better companion than them in the world. "We should give them not just water but also love because they feel love," she would remark. She went on talking whenever she came near the plants. More than her words, the way she used to be gleeful and enraptured amid the plants was exhilarating.

There were many discussions between her and me. I understood that she doesn't take any clear stand in most of them. However, she would occasionally make statements that sounded like verdicts. She used to say that discussions were useless and that talking didn't offer any solution. I would call her a pessimist. She believed that besides talking, many things happen inside our hearts. Sometimes, she seemed to be a profound person.

She used to call me Dasu. Frankly speaking, it is not my actual name. She told me that she had lost a close friend when she was in Germany and that she got the feeling of being with him in my camaraderie. But she didn't disclose his details, however much I insisted. I would ponder what type of friend he was and how close he was to her. I never saw her divulging or discussing her personal matters.

Whenever I asked her to give advice, she would say, "Dasu, whatever is apt for you, you do it." I sensed that people came near her only to a certain extent and stopped there. I could never comprehend why there were dividing lines between her and others, because she was friendly with everyone.

Visiting her house became a habit for me. Gradually, I started cherishing more and more the act of going there. Now and then, I would touch her fingers and shoulders unintentionally. That house was akin to a homestead entangled in the midst of a forest. I used to feel that the plants didn't like me going there. Sometimes, I would feel suffocated. When I revealed the same to her, she said, "You should start loving the plants. Only then they would know who their friends are and who are not." I have neither amity nor enmity towards plants. 'I am not a person of plants,' I would say. 'No person can be like that, Dasu. Go near plants and observe; they keep telling you something,' she would respond. I used to say, 'I am facing difficulty listening to humans' words. Then, why do I need the language of plants, Madam? Please leave me.'

I never had the courage or closeness to ask her questions about personal matters. I saw her guffawing only once. That day, I had an incomprehensible conversation with her. There were no photos of any person on the walls of that house. When I mentioned this, she remarked: "Isn't hanging photos on walls tantamount to flinging the persons out from our hearts?"

I said, "You could at least hang your photo."

She guffawed nonstop and replied, "You want me to throw myself out. Is that okay?"

"What is the problem in remembering people by seeing their photos?"

"What is meant by remembering? Should we remember their facial features, etc.? But what should we do by remembering like that?"

It appeared she didn't want an answer from me. I used to feel defenceless whenever she contended like that.

My aunt would say that she was a strange but nice person. Nagalakshmi Madam never asked for any help. 'There is much time for that in future,' she used to say. However, she asked for my help once.

She was going to Kerala with her friends for one week. She asked me to stay in her house to water the plants and look after the place.

"No need of staying during nights. Coming once a day at any time would suffice," she said.

Not wanting to lose the opportunity to help her, and because of the liking I had for that house, I acquiesced at once.

"I would stay until you come back," I said excitedly.

"Okay, as you wish. In that case, you can stay in the guest bedroom," she said and placed the keys of the house except that of her bedroom in my hand.

"Be wary. Befriend the plants. Exercise caution, Dasu."

I went with clothes sufficient for one week. I didn't heed the advice given by my family members. They said there was no need to stay there at night, and I could go just once a day.

I experienced a gung-ho spirit on the first day. I didn't have much work to do. I enjoyed the fish curry and the sweet dish she had prepared and kept in the fridge. I watched TV for a sufficient duration and slipped into slumber. I heard some voices of children in my sleep. I woke up early in the morning. I didn't have the habit of getting up so early. Cold wind rushed in when I opened the backdoor. I never imagined the morning would be so beautiful. That place was invigoratingly cool and serene. A thin film of tiny moisture drops was seen on the leaves; the trees seemed to be sleeping with limbs drawn in. The ground was replete with leaves, indicating strong winds the previous night. I thought the plants did not need watering.

On the second day, no sooner had I opened the window than the wind from the guava tree rushed in and rendered the room cool. I went out with my friends, loitered in town and returned. Fatigued, I went to sleep. I woke up at midnight. The room, which was cool until then, became warm. I heard the sounds of some whispers. I remained still without opening my eyes. I could not make out what those whispers were. They sounded like discussions. Who could they be? There was nothing except the plants and me. Were the trees and plants talking about me? If trees talk, what could be their language? Were they actually trees? I was scared to open my eyes.

Her words came to my mind. If we want to befriend them, we should touch every plant. Gradually, the whispers became so loud that I felt someone was shouting in my ears. My name was heard once in the middle, and I was startled. The window's panels were hitting each other due to opening and closing, making a grating noise. Am I dreaming? I thought. I opened my eyes partly to notice that blue light was falling on me. I had never seen such light before. Besides that strange light, there was a weird fragrance and sounds of whispers. I opened my eyes in one go. All the noises stopped at once, and the blue light vanished instantaneously. I got up, closed the window panes, went into the hall, switched on the TV and slept.

We think plants are nice creatures. Are all of them good, or could a few plants be bad? Which are good plants? Do they constitute those useful for humans, or the ones which help other plants? Do they identify good plants and bad plants among themselves? I was befuddled. Am I reflecting too much? There is no need for that.

The next day, I got a phone call from her. I told her everything was all right. She didn't ask many questions. She told me to be wary and snapped the connection. Whom did she tell to be careful, now? Was it to me? I thought.

That day, I watered all the plants with concern and examined them carefully. I lifted the jasmine vine that drooped listlessly and tied it to the stick at a higher level. I thought I tried to make a truce with them. I vetted every plant attentively and found they were swaying to the winds peacefully and smilingly. There were many fallen leaves on the ground. I swept all of them and threw them out. I felt I had done arduous work after many days. Then I read books with attention without going anywhere.

Before going to bed, I opened the window intrepidly. It seemed a week had elapsed since the last new moon day. Thin moonlight sneaked into the room and spread out. It was like calm before a storm. Listening to songs on the phone, I slipped into slumber.

I didn't know when I had woken up, but it was sultry, and I was perspiring. Suddenly wind has stopped. Dense blue light filled the room. I opened my eyes partly and looked. Branches of trees and shadows of leaves protruded through the window. I was frightened by the shadows. Harsh sounds and whispers were heard. They were asking me to leave.

Perhaps the jasmine vine that I straightened in the morning was touching my ear. I shuddered faintly.

I presumed those sounds gave me the power to comprehend. You are not Dasu; you have an erotic longing for her. You will not get what you are expecting. Her love is a python. If hungry, it will devour you. I opened my eyes. It was not a dream but a reality. Thick blue light surrounded me.

Do these plants know how to talk, or am I interpreting the sounds like that? Do I have lust for her? Have they known it? What happened to her friend? Did he flee, leaving everything, including her?

I know one tale: one may trust anyone except a python. However amicable it may appear, it will swallow the food when it is available.

The house that looked beautiful earlier appeared like a prison now. I peered into her bedroom through the keyhole. I could see nothing at first. Later, a small photo came into my view. With her arms around him, she was smiling. Is he Dasu? Does he resemble me, or do I look like him? There was no smile on his face. I thought a python was crawling on the photo. I was startled. I walked slowly and came out of the house. I don't remember whether I locked the door or not. I headed forward. As if all the plants and trees were jeering at me from behind, the wind was chasing me and blowing gustily.

***

Castle of Albuquerque

The first thing I noticed in him was his coppery hair. Had I not seen him in that Spanish fort, maybe I wouldn't have given much attention to him. Somehow, it seemed as though he belonged to that fort long ago. Was he a Spanish king, or a general, or a minister's son? Besides a hope, his gaze betrayed an infatuation with the fort. His eyes reminded me of those of a leopard.

The wind made his coppery hair sway, adding beauty to the surroundings. He was speaking to a Spanish lady. I could not discern the actual meaning of their words, but the purport reached me faintly. His words revealed his desire for her. Her response was a smile which hinted that she recognised and enjoyed his desire.

Appearing uninterested in them, I walked inside. Castillo de Albuquerque is a massive fort. It had a large room in the front with broad windows in a row. The setting sun was clearly visible through them. The hues of the evening were daubing a strange beauty onto the surroundings. Soon after I entered, it seemed as if the gentle breeze coming through windows has halted at once, and someone was staring at me with a fixed gaze from somewhere. Some old memories stirred in me for a few moments, as if I had visualised that beautiful sunset on many evenings in the past. I had a feeling that many people were exiting me and someone was drawing me near him. Did I belong to this place ages ago?

The man with coppery hair was calling me from afar. There was amazement in his voice. He used a peculiar name while calling me. I didn't understand the reason for it.

"Are you okay?" he asked, coming towards me.

"Yes, I am," I said, regaining composure.

"The fort will be closed soon. We need to move from here." His English sentences were breaking in the middle.

I followed him.

He asked me, "There is a small live music programme in Madrid tonight. Would you come?"

I nodded vaguely and moved out from there.

My stay here is just for one day. Yet, many things happen in a short time. The mind, the world, and people all keep changing. Perhaps we spend time as if somebody told us something, as if some force instructed us, a few signs of the past are stowed away, and a broken heart lies in a place!

Is there any cause for my coming here? Might I have wanted to come and spend time here like this, see these environs and meet a person? Had some change occurred inside me? No, nothing of that sort had taken place. The lives of humans are short-spanned. Nobody bothers much about anything. All this is but an apprehension of the heart to create a few lively moments!

He called me with a name I had never heard before. Maybe he had a vague idea of my name. It was the name someone had called me earlier. I felt an unknown astonishment. Why did he call me by that name? Had that man with coppery hair been stalking me for long?

I had never come to this place earlier. But after visiting that ancient fort, I felt some indistinct agitation in my heart. I rang my only friend Malik. I wanted to say something, but I thought it would be better if he didn't respond. Why did I think like that? I don't know. He didn't reply to my call. I heaved a sigh of relief.

I decided to go to the Madrid live music programme. I put on the purple frock, which I like most. I fastened a brownish-purple brooch to it. I affixed a small pin to my curly hair. Perhaps I stowed that attire away only for this occasion. After getting ready fully, I looked at myself in the mirror. Someone appeared faintly. Someone like me! I laughed at myself.

It seemed he had been waiting for me outside. I thought I heard him say something upon seeing me. He called me by the same name! I went and sat facing him. He was perplexed.

He said, "Isn't this your favourite colour? You are very distinct from this evening, these people, and these lights." A Spanish accent crept into his English. No desire was discernible in his compliment. The amazement that sounded in his words remained intact.

"Your coppery hair is setting you apart from others," I said.

I didn't know whether I couched a compliment in that sentence or if I simply meant that his hair was the reason I recognised him first.

"What are you?" I asked.

He smiled and replied, "Shall we spend this evening without any such questions?" His eyes looked special, like those of a leopard. His smile seemed to stymie show of authority.

"Will you have wine, princess?"

Seeing the smile on my face, he ordered it even before I replied.

I asked him directly, "Why have you called me here?"

"I thought you would listen to the music." His voice didn't betray his actual intention, I thought.

A Spanish song was playing. It sounded like folk music.

"It is not a song of the present time," he said.

I tried to listen to that music and glanced at him as if I didn't like it.

"In fact, I called you here to relate a story," he said and started his narration. He didn't wait for my assent.

"Today, when I observed you watching the sunset, I saw Ines de Castro in you."

It was the same name that had echoed weirdly and faintly in his voice a few hours ago.

"Whose name is it?" I asked.

After sipping the wine, he began his tale.

"She is called 'The Death Queen.' She belonged to the 14th century. Her actual name was Ines de Castro. The Prince of Portugal, Pedro, loved her. He was head over heels in love with her, so lost in it that he forgot himself. His father, King Alfonso, didn't approve of his love. He tried to change his son's mind in many ways. However, Pedro refused to leave her. So, the king had her assassinated."

After pausing a little, he took a deep breath in and continued, "This is sounding like an ordinary love story, isn't it? Pedro became king two years after his father's death. He had Ines de Castro's corpse exhumed and gave it regal status by placing it on the royal throne. He made all the people of his country acknowledge her as queen by announcing that he had married her when she was alive. He even made everyone kiss the skeleton's hand. Then, he apprehended those who killed her and had their hearts prised out in public. Thus, Ines de Castro became the queen of death." He concluded the story.

Looking at me fondly, he said, "I like your wheat-hued body, honey eyes, and black tresses immensely." He drew out his hand to touch my hair, but soon drew his hand back.

After remaining silent for long, I asked, "Do you say Pedro's love was noble?"

"Don't know," he replied.

"The killer of Ines must have seen her inordinate beauty."

"Maybe he killed her only after seeing it." There was consternation in him.

After some time, he said, "You are not drinking any wine." He moved the glass towards me.

"Often, rocks and walls are left as witnesses to stories," I said, taking the glass.

He remained quiet.

Why had I come at his invitation, even though he was a stranger to me? I wondered. He might tell any stories – I should leave at once, I felt strongly. But his glance was stopping me from leaving.

He said, "Will you dance with me?"

"No, I don't know how to dance," I peered into his eyes.

"Why are you looking into my eyes repeatedly?" He asked.

"Your eyes are like those of a leopard. I feel I saw them somewhere."

"It is said that eyes represent one's soul," he said with surprise.

"Is that so? Then, are you a hunting soul?"

He sipped wine calmly. Somehow, I slowly began to feel troubled in his presence.

I got up suddenly and said, "I will leave now."

"Sit with me for some time, princess," he said, almost beseechingly.

After relating that story, he didn't smile like before. He was calm.

He took my hand into his. His hand was warm and soft. I felt his breath in his touch. Dense darkness pervaded around. Stars were shining in the sky. Stars too, sometimes reveal history.

"Perhaps Prince Pedro did that not to project his love as noble but to fulfil her wish of becoming queen." He took out a photo from a book and showed it to me.

Ines de Castro, the queen of death, in a purple frock, on the throne! Someone was kissing the hand of her skeleton. I felt a shudder inside me upon seeing that photo. Unable to come out of the shock, I looked at my purple frock.

"I will go now." I got up and walked quickly.

He followed me. While scurrying, my leg hit some object, and I was about to trip. He caught hold of my hand tightly and prevented me from falling. Suddenly, he bent down on one knee and kissed my hand.

"What is your name?"

"Alvaro Goncalves."

I recollected the sentence he had shown in the book:

The three noble men, appointed by King Alfonso – Pero Coelho, Alvaro Goncalves, and Diogo Lopes Pacheo – went to the Monastery of Santa Clara-a-Velha in Coimbra, in the gardens where she and Pedro used to meet and killed Ines by decapitating her.

***

Celestial

I recalled the day I had met Alten for the first time.

He brought Sifu. With large ears, big eyes and a smooth head with not a single hair on it, Sifu looked very odd. His appearance reminded me of a small rabbit with long ears. I gave Alten an application form and asked him to write all the details in it.

He carried out my instructions carefully. However, he left the column against family name blank.

I said, "This too has to be filled up."

"We don't have them. The name of our tribe is Ovog. Shall I write it?" he asked. He showed documents showing Sifu was his nephew. I had no reason to suspect anything in him.

The parents of the wards in my day-care centre were all doing big jobs. People in that area had great trust in me and my centre. They say I look after the kids well. I don't admit all children into my centre but choose them carefully. I take them only if everything is right for me.

Alten looked a quiet and uncomplicated person. He came to work as a casual, temporary labourer for a bridge construction nearby. He said someone had told him about my centre, and he came searching for it.

At first, I was not willing to get Sifu admitted to my centre. I didn't like Alten's poverty and his appearance. Moreover, it would be a problem not only with the habits of low-class children like him but also their language. They don't usually mix well with other kids, nor obey the instructions given. Perhaps I have a greater dislike for their cheap mentality than their language or habits. Whenever I said these words, Shanthi would get piqued. She used to chide me saying, "Ammu, how do you get such notions? Stop thinking like an average Indian first, particularly about children,"

But I had no discomfort whatsoever in thinking like that. Have the kids come from heaven? I find children extremely selfish. Why this "Indian" in her sentence?

I strongly believe that one cannot survive here unless he or she identifies certain values, at least appears to be respecting them and behaves accordingly. I have no qualms in admitting this. I am an ostentatious, high-class person who looks flamboyant but gentle.

Usually, I stringently deny admission if I don't like any child, but I could not easily turn down Sifu. I thought it would be nice if Alten left without admitting him.

I said, "There are many rules and methods here, all of which have to be followed strictly. If your child doesn't conform to them, we will throw him out of here. Particularly, his habits should be good. You should collect him on time in the evenings. Else, an extra fee will be charged, which will be calculated per hour." I found my own voice contemptible while uttering these sentences.

"You mentioned all these things in the application form and took my signature on it. Where is the need to explain them to me?" Alten said with a smile on his face.

"Did you go through all of them thoroughly?" However much I tried to conceal it, the derision in my voice was perceivable. That, perhaps, is my baseness.

"I haven't read them all. But Sifu will be safe in your centre. I have no problem to put signatures on papers."

I understood that Alten was determined to join Sifu in my centre.

"What does Sifu eat usually?"

"He doesn't eat anything except raw beans and boiled peas. If he does not want to mingle with other kids, please don't force him to befriend them against his wish. He does any work only if he likes it."

I wanted to say categorically, "Then he doesn't fit here well. Take him back." But Alten hastened to add quickly: "He does obey even if not interested. But he won't sleep at night. He looks disconsolate the whole night and glances at the stars incessantly. Tears flow continuously from his eyes. Then it will be very difficult to pacify him."

Does Sifu belong to a special category, I wondered. I wanted not to come to any decision without observing him thoroughly.

*

I noticed some change in children at my centre after Sifu came. Their crying and shouting, which used to cause a din, had diminished. No kid would quarrel with Sifu. Even boisterous and querulous children were calm near Sifu. He had very large ears. In the last six months, the occasions when Sifu talked were very few. Sometimes, with a smile on his face, he would mingle with other children and play nicely. However, he would frequently sit by the window and look outside. The parents of children gave me feedback of late, saying their kids were happy and not making much tumult at home. They praised me on and off.

Sifu would never eat any other food except what Alten brought in a box. When someone said anything to him, he would smile and nod his head either across or vertically.

Alten told me that they hailed from Magnolia. He was found by Alten's daughter at a Buddhist temple. My liking for Sifu had increased.

One day, I had to go out for some work. I asked Katy to look after the children until I returned. Just an hour later, there was a call from Katy requesting me to come at once. She was very perturbed. When I went there, I saw all the children dancing naked around Sifu, holding one another's hands. Sifu was in the centre, making some sounds. That scene was alarming. I was scared to go near the children. I remained calm and still for a few minutes. "Sifu," I screamed. The children looked weary and fell down. Sifu looked at me intently with a fixed gaze. His eyes appeared as though they had been here for aeons, filled times immemorial and stowing the entire world in them. For a few moments, my surroundings and I came to a standstill. I scampered as if disturbed by a loud sound in my sleep. I put outfits on all the children. Sifu was staring in the same manner. He looked like a hermit ripe with life's experiences. Is he an ascetic in the form of a child?

*

The parents of the children all came one by one and took their kids. Katy, too, left as if nothing had happened. Alten hasn't come yet. Only Sifu and I were left. Sifu came, stood in front of me and gestured that he needed water. I gave him water.

I waited for Alten. He didn't come, though it was past seven. I tried to talk to him on the phone. However, the call could not be connected. I didn't know what to do with Sifu. I decided to take him with me for that night.

"Alten hasn't come. You have to stay with me tonight," I said to Sifu. He accompanied me silently. My house is adjacent to my day-care centre. I boiled peas and gave them to him. I tried to talk with him. He appeared sad. I tried to console him by saying that Alten will definitely come the next morning.

I opened the door to the balcony and sat there with a cup of black coffee.

I recalled the incident that had occurred at the centre. When I saw Sifu in that state, there was some agitation in me. I felt there was some supernatural power in him. The sound coming from his mouth was weird.

The sound of a moving truck afar was heard. People, usually, don't venture out into the freezing cold. Thin darkness prevailed outside. Stars were seen in the sky here and there. A meteorite was hurtling fast in the sky. Sifu came abruptly and placed his palms on my eyes for one minute, and then took them off. I could figure out that he didn't want me to see meteors falling.

I remembered reading somewhere that Mongolians consider watching a falling meteorite a bad omen.

Sifu stood beside me. Sadness had disappeared from his eyes. His small shadow of light was visible in my lap. In such a situation, it is a great experience to have a friend beside you savouring the infinite darkness, cold, and silence.

I took Sifu into my bedroom, put him to sleep and came back.

*

What should I do if Alten doesn't come? Could he have met with an accident? I pondered for some time. Alten, too, cannot be forgotten once we see him. He looks like a wayfarer lost in some country and came to this one. Such is his demeanour, too. He analyses any issue in and out and explains thoroughly. Half of his words, however, cannot be understood easily.

One day, I said to Alten smilingly, "Children tell different kinds of lies. They pretend to be hungry or to be in pain. Sifu, however, never even talks."

"Perhaps children don't know that that is called fibbing. But a lie doesn't become a truth," he said shrugging his shoulders queerly.

Even before I could ask him why he was late picking up Sifu, he would resort to such prolonged talk and leave with the boy! It became a habit for me to wait for his words when he came late in the evenings. It even progressed to having coffee in my centre.

I closed the door of the balcony gently in order to avoid noise and came to Sifu. He was asleep. I sat beside him and placed my hand on his head.

I got a feeling that some energy was coming out from his head; light, darkness, peace and unrest were overflowing. I felt that I was being removed from myself. The thick layer that had been covering me for so long seemed to have broken. I saw myself coming out naked and bouncing. My body hardened like a snowball and could not be moved. Thin, blue light spread in the entire room.

I removed my hand and hopped out of the room. I was drenched in sweat. The clock showed five in the morning. What kind of experience was this?! I sat near Sifu for a long time. I didn't know what had happened, but I felt light. I felt as if I had gotten rid of a longstanding burden. Never had I felt such lightness before. I was reminded of my mother's words: "Ammu, there are no ethereal experiences separately. Those we are supposed to experience come to us. We must experience them."

***

Blue Comet

"He used to draw pictures on papers for me and tell stories about stars. He would sing lullabies to put me to sleep. We used to pick coloured stones together along the river. I never saw him crossing my village's frontiers. Why did such a man, Param, flee the village?"

"His family members say that it is because of the girl he loved. According to them, a change occurred in him after he met her."

"Hmm, he used to get crushed between pain and sadness from the beginning. Perhaps they made him leave the village."

"It may not be because of that, Saavi. He used to think excessively about life. Once, he told me about a comet. 'People who sight them know the secrets of the universe,' he would say. He strongly believed in them"

"So, are you saying that Param saw the blue comet? Did he disappear because of that alone? But what are these secrets of the universe? Would anyone disappear after seeing it?"

"I don't know, Saavi."

*

"Subbu, you are on your second peg. The story you told is enough. Let us go home. Turn your vehicle."

"Shut up. It is not a story but reality. Let us proceed. I am not getting any kick even after drinking rum."

"Did you love her?"

"I don't know if it is love or something else. But I haven't seen any person like her anywhere. She would talk with birds, trees and animals. Her words seemed like tete-a-tete. Coming to humans, she was very compassionate with them. Whenever a person died in the village, she would go and weep along with them and pour coins beside the corpse. I think she believed that I was harmless and trusted me. Occasionally, she would come at midnight, wake me up and say, 'Shall we go to the river?' I used to go with her and sit on the riverbank. She, who always used to talk about something, was silent at those times and would look into the dark sky. Sometimes she swam nonstop and then sat beside me. I never felt like touching her despite her sitting naked by my side. She was a part of Nature. I cherished those occasions, for I felt that peace was spreading inside me slowly. My heart used to become very light."

"With her, did you have any ...?"

"You, dirty .... Stop it."

"Okay. Let us leave it. But at least tell me where she has gone."

"There were numerous rumours that she eloped with someone, went to another city for roles in movies, went abroad for higher studies ... and so on.

"Did you search for her any time?"

"You can't get her by searching. Only if she wants, will she come back."

"Why did she leave?"

"I don't know. But she was not seen after I told her a story about a blue comet."

"Did she sight the blue comet?"

"I don't know."

*

The bus went past a hillock and stopped by the side of a valley. I disembarked from the bus. The path that leads to that village goes straight into the valley. One has to walk for five kilometres to reach the village.

I stopped in front of a tin-roofed house. The door was bolted from the inside. I knocked on it. A man came from inside and looked at me.

"Are you Saidulu?"

Saying "Yes, *amma*," he brought a small indigenous wooden cot from inside and placed it in the open place.

Shadows of tall trees and the delectable atmosphere made the place cool.

He brought a crude stool made of wicker and sat on it.

"Nobody has come for him all these days. We have been waiting for a long time," Saidulu said.

“Where does he stay?”

“He doesn’t stay here, amma. He keeps roaming in the forest. If he comes any time, I cook some rice and give it to him. He eats it only if he likes it; else, he throws it away. He doesn’t talk but mumbles to himself. However, he doesn’t look like a lunatic. He plays for some time with kids. Shepherds of this area say that he can be spotted in the caves of Gabbilala Dibba.

“How should we go there?”

“Do you want to meet him? I am not sure he will allow you to go near him. “

“Why?”

“He doesn’t let women near him. If they try, he hurls stones at them. Mumbling to himself, he moves his hands in the air.”

“Why?” I think something obstructed my throat. My question sounded as if I was trying to swallow it.

“Don’t know, amma. What relation is he to you?”

I didn’t know what to say. I only told him that I wanted to visit him.

Saidulu grumbled to himself and said, “It is now late evening. You can go tomorrow in the morning. Stay back here tonight.”

I said, “I will sleep outside.”

He didn't allow me to sleep outside, saying animals keep prowling around at night. He gave cooked rice and hot soup on a plate. I felt as though I was eating after fasting for a long time. The soup was a bit pungent and bitter. Yet, I found it very tasty.

Saidulu didn't ask anything about me. I longed for sleeping outside in the night seeing the stars in the sky. I woke up at midnight. Some wild animal seemed to be howling. There were sounds of someone walking amid the trees. I wanted to call Saidulu, but pretended courage without opening my eyes.

I didn't know when I slipped into slumber again. I woke up after daybreak. Saidulu was cooking some food.

I tried to recall if I had dreamt last night, but I could recollect nothing. Vaguely, I felt that I may have dreamt.

My grandmother used to say, "We meet some people somewhere, at some place. They, who came near us, go away far from us – so far that we don't even remember them. We feel their existence in the dreams that we don't remember well." Remembering her words, I became animated.

"Today, I will go to Gabbilala Dibba," I told Saidulu.

"I will accompany you. Let us have some porridge and go."

"I don't have much time. I need to go home. So, I have to meet him today," I said.

Handing over the bowl of porridge to me, he said, "We cannot see him unless he approves of it." I drank all the porridge without saying anything.

Saidulu brought a scimitar from inside. We walked in a mud track for some distance. There was no path yonder. There were tall, thick bushes around. It was very difficult for me to walk. Saidulu, however, paced fast. We encountered a big mound. We stopped there for some time.

Saidulu said, "We have to be wary here; wild animals frequent this place," and gave me a stick.

Saidulu was wearing no footwear, yet he walked deftly. It became too arduous for me to negotiate a rocky hillock. We walked for two hours like that. I told Saidulu to give a short break. The hillock looked not big from a distance, but it was taking too long a time to negotiate it.

"How did he come here?"

"Venkusa brought him. Venkusa is like a venerated mentor for all of us here. One day, he brought this man and left him here. He was found in Varanasi, he said. Venkusa told us not to chide him but to give him food whenever he comes here."

We reached a place where the ground was flat. It was cool there, with the shadow of a big tree. Gasping, I suggested to him that we stop a bit there.

"Shall I tell you something, amma? However much we scout for him here, we won't see him. Many people talk about the caves of Gabbilala Dibba here as stories. They say nobody can surmise how many they are, none would return after entering them, and many cannot ever reach them despite walking a lot."

His words seemed strange; they did not look like lies.

I sat under the tree, leaning against a boulder. Saidulu was a little away from me. He lit a cigar. Soon, its smoke had spread into the air.

Snow was congealing on the smoke and turning the ground into a wetland. A small baby was walking on it and glancing at me by turning back. While she ran, the ice behind her was melting. My heart beat fast. I looked with trepidation into the sky. A blue comet dazzled in the sky, replete with smoke and ice. All of a sudden, I heard a sound similar to snoring. I looked in that direction. From the hillock in front of me, a man with wolf's eyes was hurtling towards me with a fixed gaze. I didn't have any idea where Saidulu had gone. I wanted to shout, but my mouth wouldn't open. Wind blew fast, as if someone was chasing it. I couldn't comprehend what was happening. My bag slipped from my hand and rolled. The papers and coloured stones that I stowed in it began to scatter.

I woke up with a loud scream and opened my eyes.

Saidulu was rushing towards me.

Was it a dream, reality, fright or an illusion?

He said we must go back as it may rain soon. Without saying a word, I returned. I told him I would go back to my home.

"Where from did you come, amma?" he asked.

"From a snow land that is faraway."

"Do you know his name?"

"Param."

"Your name?"

"Saavi."

"You are going back without meeting him."

"Now, there is no need to meet him."

"What relation he is to you?"

"I don't know!"

***

Notes:

Amma: A term used for addressing a woman or girl